Watts Phillips

Not Guilty

A drama, in four acts

Watts Phillips

Not Guilty
A drama, in four acts

ISBN/EAN: 9783337343774

Printed in Europe, USA, Canada, Australia, Japan

Cover: Foto ©Andreas Hilbeck / pixelio.de

More available books at **www.hansebooks.com**

DE WITT'S ACTING PLAYS.

(Number 84.)

NOT GUILTY.

A DRAMA, IN FOUR ACTS.

By WATTS PHILLIPS, Esq.

Author of "The Dead Heart," "Ticket of Leave," "Nobody's Child,"
"Maud's Peril," "Lost in London," etc., etc.

AS FIRST PERFORMED AT THE QUEEN'S THEATRE, LONG
ACRE, (UNDER THE MANAGEMENT OF MR. W. H.
LISTON,) MONDAY, FEBRUARY 22D, 1869.

TO WHICH ARE ADDED

A description of the Costume—Cast of the Characters—Entrances and Exits—
Relative Positions of the Performers on the Stage, and
the whole of the Stage Business.

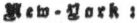

New-York:

ROBERT M. DE WITT, PUBLISHER,

No. 33 Rose Street.

DE WITT'S ACTING PLAYS.

☞ *Please notice that nearly all the Comedies, Farces and Comediettas in the following list of* DE WITT'S ACTING PLAYS" *are very suitable for representation in small Amateur Theatres and on Parlor Stages, as they need but little extrinsic aid from complicated scenery or expensive costumes. They have attained their deserved popularity by their droll situations, excellent plots, great humor and brilliant dialogues, no less than by the fact that they are the most perfect in every respect of any edition of plays ever published either in the United States or Europe, whether as regards purity of the text, accuracy and fulness of stage directions and scenery, or elegance of typography and clearness of printing.*

*** *In ordering please copy the figures at the commencement of each piece, which indicate the number of the piece in* "DE WITT'S LIST OF ACTING PLAYS."

☞ *Any of the following Plays sent, postage free on- receipt of price—15 cents each.*

Address,

ROBERT M. DE WITT,
No. 33 Rose Street, New York.

☞ The figure following the name of the Play denotes the number of Acts. The figures in the columns indicate the number of characters—M. *male*; F. *female.*

No.		M.	F.
75.	Adrienne, drama, 3 acts	7	3
114.	Anything for a Change, comedy, 1	3	3
167.	Apple Blossoms, comedy, 3 acts	7	3
93.	Area Belle (The), farce, 1 act	3	2
40.	Atchi, comedietta, 1 act	3	2
89.	Aunt Charlotte's Maid, farce, 1 act	3	3
192.	Game of Cards (A), comedietta, 1	3	1
166.	Bardell vs. Pickwick, sketch, 1 act.	6	2
41.	Beautiful Forever, farce, 1 act	2	3
141.	Bells (The), drama, 3 acts	9	3
67.	Birthplace of Podgers, farce, 1 act.	7	3
36.	Black Sheep, drama, 3 acts	7	5
160.	Blow for Blow, drama, 4 acts	11	6
70.	Bonnie Fish Wife, farce, 1 act	3	1
179.	Breach of Promise,, drama, 2 acts.	5	2
25.	Broken-Hearted Club, comedietta, 1	4	8
24.	Cabman, No. 93, farce, 1 act	2	2
1.	Caste, comedy, 3 acts	5	3
69.	Caught by the Cuff, farce, 1 act	4	1
175.	Cast upon the World, drama, 5 acts.	10	5
55.	Catharine Howard, historical play, 3 acts	12	3
80.	Charming pair, farce, 1 act	4	3
65.	CheckMate, comedy, 2 acts	6	5
68.	Chevalier de St. George, drama, 3	9	3
76.	Chops of the Channel, farce, 1 act.	3	2
149.	Clouds, comedy, 4 acts	8	7
121.	Comical Countess, farce, 1 act	3	1
107.	Cupboard Love, farce, 1 act	2	1
152.	Cupid's Eye-Glass, comedy, 1 act	1	1
52.	Cup of Tea, comedietta, 1 act	3	1
148.	Cut off with a Shilling, comedietta, 1 act	2	1
113.	Cyril's Success, comedy, 5 acts	10	4
199.	Captain of the Watch (The), comedietta, 1 act	4	2
20.	Daddy Gray, drama, 3 acts	8	4
4.	Dandelion's Dodges, farce, 1 act	4	2
22.	David Garrick, comedy, 3 acts	8	3
96.	Dearest Mamma, comedietta, 1 act,	4	3
16.	Dearer than Life, drama, 3 acts	6	5
58.	Deborah (Leah) drama, 3 acts	7	6
125.	Deerfoot, farce. 1 act	5	1
71.	Doing for the Best, drama, 2 acts	5	3
142.	Dollars and Cents, comedy, 3 acts.	9	4
No.		M.	F.
21.	Dreams, drama, 5 acts	6	3
186.	Duchesse de la Valliere, play, 5 acts.	6	4
47.	Easy Shaving, farce, 1 act	5	2
13.	Everybody's Friend, comedy, 3 acts.	6	5
200.	Estranged, an operetta, 1 act	2	1
103.	Faust and Marguerite, drama, 3 acts,	9	7
9.	Fearful Tragedy in the Seven Dials, interlude, 1 act	4	1
128.	Female Detective, drama, 3 acts	11	4
101.	Fernande, drama, 3 acts	11	10
99.	Fifth Wheel, comedy, 3 acts	10	2
145.	First Love, comedy, 1 act	4	1
102.	Foiled, drama, 4 acts	9	3
88.	Founded on Facts, farce, 1 act	4	2
74.	Garrick Fever, farce, 1 act	7	4
53.	Gertrude's Money Box, farce, 1 act.	4	2
73.	Golden Fetter (Fettered), drama, 3	11	4
30.	Goose with the Golden Eggs, farce, 1 act	5	3
131.	Go to Putney, farce, 1 act	4	3
28.	Happy Pair, comedietta, 1 act	1	1
151.	Hard Case (A), farce, 1 act	2	
8.	Henry Dunbar, drama, 4 acts	10	3
180.	Henry the Fifth, historical play, 5	38	5
19.	He's a Lunatic, farce, 1 act	3	2
60.	Hidden Hand, drama, 4 acts	5	5
187.	His Own Enemy, farce, 1 act	4	1
174.	Home, comedy, 3 acts	4	3
64.	Household Fairy, sketch, 1 act	1	1
190.	Hunting the Slipper, farce, 1 act	4	1
191.	High C, comedietta, 1 act	4	2
197.	Hunchback (The), play, 5 acts	14	2
18.	If I Had a Thousand a Year, farce, 1 act	4	3
116.	I'm Not Mesilf at All, original Irish stew, 1 act	3	2
129.	In for a Holiday, farce, 1 act	2	3
159.	In the Wrong House, farce, 1 act	4	2
122.	Isabella Orsini, drama, 4 acts	11	4
177.	I Shall Invite the Major, comedy, 1	4	1
100.	Jack Long, drama, 2 acts	9	2
139.	Joy is Dangerous, comedy, 2 acts	3	3
17.	Kind to a Fault, comedy, 2 acts	6	4
86.	Lady of Lyons, play, 5 acts	12	5
72.	Lame Excuse, farce, 1 act	4	2

NOT GUILTY.

A Drama,

IN FOUR ACTS.

By WATTS PHILLIPS, Esq.,

Author of " *The Dead Heart,*" " *Ticket of Leave,*" " *Nobody's Child,*" " *Maud's Peril,*'
" *Lost in London,*" " *A Golden Fetter,*" *etc., etc.*

AS FIRST PERFORMED AT THE QUEEN'S THEATER, LONG ACRE,
UNDER THE MANAGEMENT OF MR. W. H. LISTON,
ON MONDAY, FEBRUARY 22, 1869.

TO WHICH IS ADDED

A DESCRIPTION OF THE COSTUMES—CAST OF THE CHARACTERS—EN-
TRANCES AND EXITS—RELATIVE POSITIONS OF THE PER-
FORMERS ON THE STAGE, AND THE WHOLE
OF THE STAGE BUSINESS.

———

NEW YORK:
ROBERT M. DE WITT, PUBLISHER,

CAST OF CHARACTERS.

Queen's Theatre,
Long Acre, Feb. 22, 1869.

Captain Willoughby. }
Silas Jarrett.   } ....Mr. S. EMERY.
Jack Snipe...Mr. J. L. TOOLE.
Triggs..Mr. L. BROUGH.
Trumble..Mr. J. HOWARD.
Mr. St. Clair..Mr. JOHN CLAYTON.
Robert Arnold.......................................Mr. HENRY IRVING.
Polecat..Mr. C. SEYTON.
Isaac Vidler...Mr. W. STEPHENS.
Wattles..Mr. H. MELLON.
Governor...Mr. KEET WEBB.

Policemen, Bakers, Recruits, Jailers, Villagers, Convicts, Warders, Officers, Soldiers, etc., etc.

Margaret Armitage...........}
Alice Armitage (her Daughter.) } ....Miss HENRIETTA HODSON.
Polly..Miss H. EVERARD.
Mrs. McTavish..Miss EWELL.
Ladies...{ Miss SUTHERLAND.
                                                     { Miss NORMAN.
                                                     { Miss ST. CLAIR.

*.*The main incidents of this drama, as connected with Silas Jarrett, is a FACT recorded in one of the most celebrated of criminal trials.

PROGRAMME OF SCENERY.

ACT I.—1847.

SCENE I —A STREET IN SOUTHAMPTON.
THE BAR GATE.

SCENE II.—INTERIOR OF A GARRET.

SCENE III —A PORTION OF SOUTHAMPTON DOCKS.
SCENE IV.—OUTWARD BOUND.
THE MADRAS BOAT.

ACT II.

THE QUARRIES AT DARTMOOR.
THE CONVICTS.

ACT III.—INDIA, 1857.

SCENE I.—BHURTPOOR.

A Military Post and Trading Out-Station on the Banks of the Jumna.
SCENE II.—INTERIOR OF VERANDAH IN MR. ST. CLAIR'S BUNGALOW.
SCENE III.—A DESERTED BATTLE FIELD (INDIA.)

ACT IV.

OAKFIELD GRANGE (NEAR SOUTHAMPTON)

SCENERY.

ACT I.—*Scene* I.—Southampton Bar.

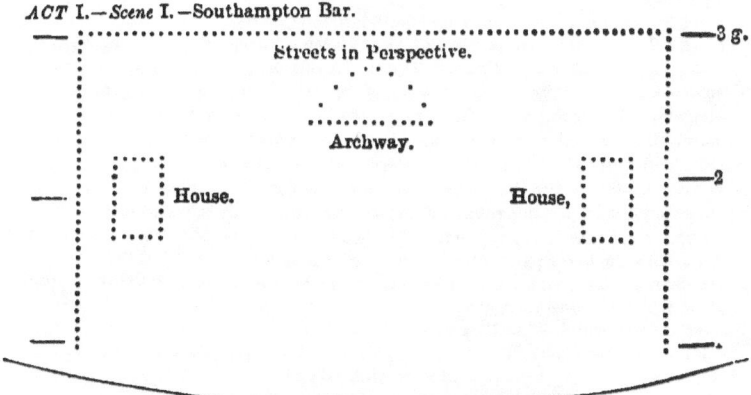

Archway c., backed by streets in perspective. Act opens upon a corner of a street in Southampton; R. and L. of 2d grooves, two houses built out—one L., a military rendezvous and recruiting house, called, "The Iron Duke, kept by J. Dobbs," the sign representing the Wellington effigy. The walls of the "public" bear the usual recruiting post bills—"Fine Young Men Wanted," "Who'll serve the Queen!" etc.; the other house, R., forming corner of a street, is a well-to-do looking middle-class residence. On the door is a large plate, upon which appears the name of "Trumble, Solicitor." As the curtain rises to the tune of the "British Grenadiers' WATTLES, a recruiting sergeant, is discovered fixing a huge bunch of ribbons on a COUNTRYMAN's hat. TRIGGS, POLLY DOBBS, and others, male and female, looking on a GIRL pouring out liquor. Some SOLDIERS are lounging about the door, and a semi-drunken band, consisting of a DRUMMER and a FIFER, are playing at intervals —while through the large open French window of TRUMBLE's house, first floor, R., (this window must be so constructed that the action going on within the room is visible to the entire Audience.)

ACT I.—*Scene* II.—Interior of a Garret, miserably furnished.

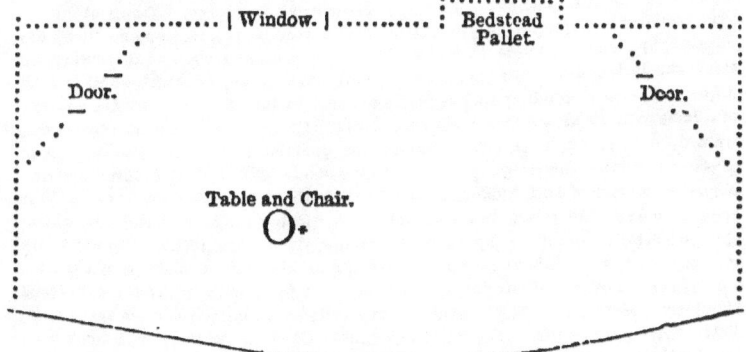

The bare walls blotched with damp—the ceiling showing the rafters in places. Door, R. (diagonal.) Another door, L., half glazed, leads to an inner room. Window at back, R. C., looks out into a narrow street, and upon the parapet of opposite house. The furniture of the room consists of a chair, a table, a candlestick, in which about

an inch of candle is burning, and a pallet bed, in recess in L. flat. On the bed
ALICE, a child of about six years old, is lying, covered by a ragged counterpane.
Moonlight.

ACT I.—*Scene* III.—A portion of the Southampton Docks. Steamer bell ringing.

ACT I.—*Scene* IV.—A portion of the interior of a sleeping cabin on board the
"Begum," packet ship to Madras. The ship is seen lengthways. The scene divided,
so as to show in perspective the elevation of the poop, with mast, sail, rigging, lifeboat,
etc., etc. MAN at the wheel, OFFICER OF THE WATCH near him ; the latter nodding
asleep. On the level of the stage, the whole interior of cabin is visible, berths on each
side, ladder ascending to poop-deck, stern portholes showing the rippling sea, which
is also visible beyond the poop-decks in a shimmer of moonlight. Cabin table,
chairs, etc., as in passenger boat of the second class. A table, beneath the usual
swing lamp, SILAS JARRETT seated, his head is uncovered, showing a bush of red
hair, while the lower part of his face is concealed by a thick beard of the same color.
He wears a loose great coat Two bottles are on table, and he is drinking from a
glass, which he constantly refills.

ACT II.—*Scene* I.—The Quarries at Dartmoor.

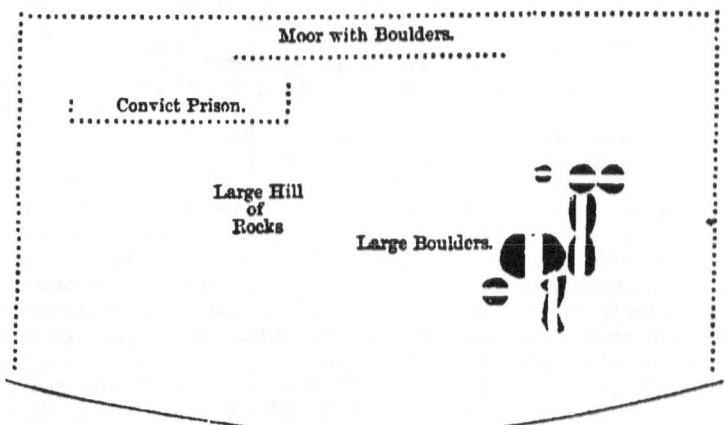

The convict prison in middle distance, R. In the extreme distance a vast extent of
moor, wild and undulating, with large boulder rocks or tors. Down stage, L.
huge boulders of slate, partially worked, a rough road is quarried among them, descending by a gentle incline to stage. To R., near C., and somewhat further up
stage, the dark boulders rise into a sort of hill, from the top of which another road
is quarried, also descending amidst rock and ferns to and off stage. On the summit
of this heap of rocks, stunted trees with other varieties of wild, coarse vegetation ;
framed, so to speak, by this foreground ; the quarries stretch out behind, full of
caves and crevices, towering up or descending suddenly into deep fissures, old and
neglected workings half hidden by the hardy herbage which clings even to these
rugged rocks. The prison is on a height. A gloomy range of buildings, which,
though distant, dominates by its very presence, the savage scene. CONVICTS are
grouped everywhere about at work, quarrying or wheeling off slate in red trucks,
under the guard of WARDENS, in dark blue uniform, with white metal buttons
(frock-coat, leather belt, black varnished cap.) Some of these WARDENS carry muskets, others wear swords. The " Good Conduct " CONVICTS wear loose, a frock with
knickerbockers and coarse woollen stockings, all of a dirty blue with pink stripes.
The " Bad Characters," B. C., are clad in drab and black parti-color, and they work
with a belt fastened round the waist under the frock. All have the tunic cut frock,

with buttons in front, knickerbockers of same pattern—the B. C., " Bad Conduct," have one knickerbocker of black, the other drab, ditto stockings—the caps, more like those of the Chasseurs d'Afrique than the Glengarry, are of the same stuff as frock, with same stripes—the boots strongly made highlows. The CONVICTS carry various quarrying tools, picks, &c. As curtain rises, ROBERT ARNOLD, in "good conduct" dress is discovered at work, L.

ACT III.– *Scene* I.—Bhurtpoor, a military post and trading out-station on the banks of the Jumna.

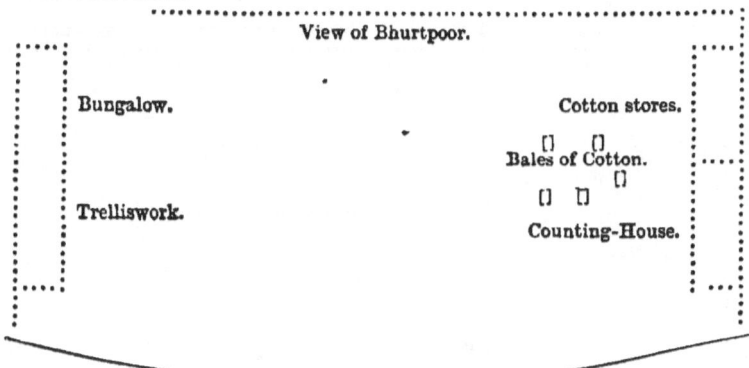

View of Bhurtpoor.

Bungalow.

Trelliswork.

Cotton stores.

Bales of Cotton.

Counting-House.

R., exterior of bungalow belonging to MR. ST. CLAIR—verandah, etc., of light trellis, and relieved by a profusion of creeping plants in flower. L., exterior of counting-houses and cotton stores. Two or three NATIVES busy marking cotton bales, etc. At back, view of the cantonment of Bhurtpoor. The extreme distance (painted cloth), the Jumna, bright with sunshine and gay with boats.

ACT III.—*Scene* II.—Interior of MR. ST. CLAIR's Bungalow—the sun-blind of verandah down c.

ACT III.—*Scene* III.—A deserted battle-field in the neighborhood of Bhurtpoor.

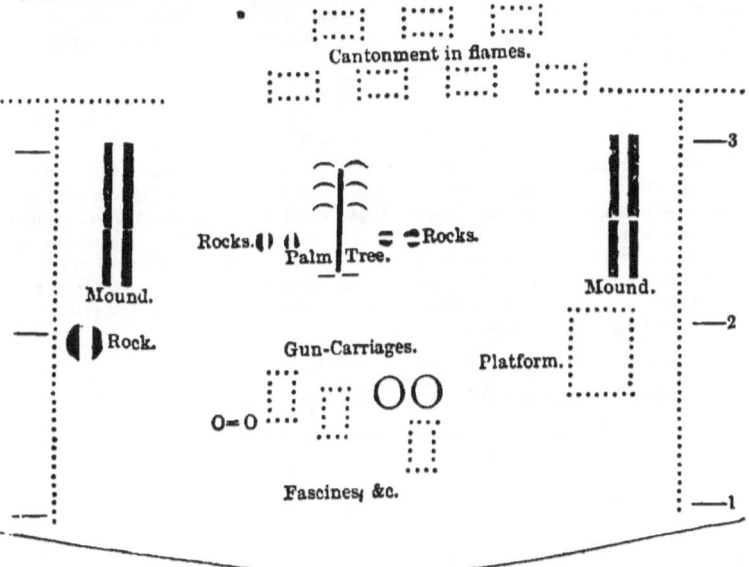

Cantonment in flames.

—3

Rocks.   Rocks.
Palm Tree.

Mound.

Mound.

—2

Rock.

Gun-Carriages.

Platform.

O=O

Fascines, &c.

—1

In foreground, some broken gun-carriages, fascines, and other military debris. In extreme distance, the cantonment in flames—in middle distance a confused mass of oriental vegetation, interspersed with blocks of stone etc., above which a feathery palm rears its tall and graceful head—a piece of rock, n. 2 E.—platform raking from L. 2 E. to nearly c. of stage. Mound of earth behind 2d grooves, and rising to back of stage with platforms raked to go off at L. U. E. and M. U. E. The firing, which has been heard at intervals, grows more and more distant, then dies utterly away as ROBERT ARNOLD and JACK SNIPE enter down raking piece from L. 2d grooves—the latter wildly excited.

ACT IV.—*Scene* I.—Oakfield Grange, MR. ST. CLAIR's house. near Southampton.

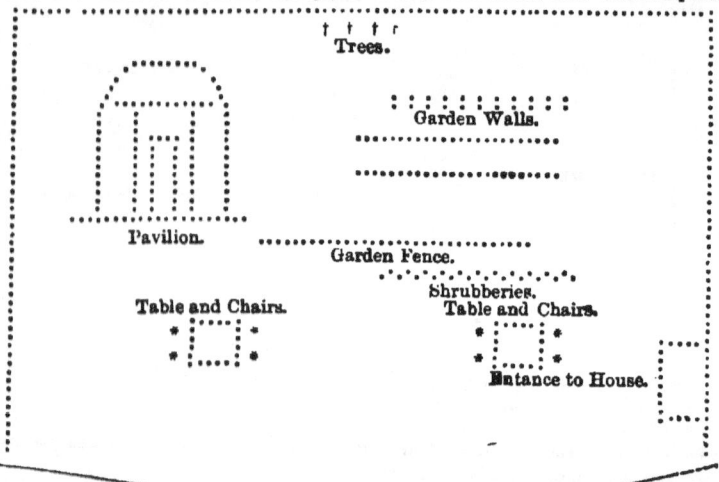

Picturesque entrance to house, L.—small pavilion, R. U. E. Shrubberies, masking garden walks, L. C.—gates on country road—towards R there is a garden fence—a small wicket gate, this gate, like the larger gates, is open—at extreme back, trees, above which is seen ivy-clad tower of church—garden tables R. and L., with chairs—bird on table, M.

PROPERTIES.

Bunch of ribbons; basket of tools; pots of ale; legal papers; matches, to light; half crown; candlestick and short candle; locksmith's tools; candle; jug of water; basket of provisions; pocket-book, full of notes and papers; ten pound note; five pound note; handcuffs; portmanteau; trucks with baggage—brown paper parcel; two bottles; wine-glass; pistol; knife; bank-notes;red wig, and red beard; red trucks for CONVICTS to carry stones on; muskets; swords; picks, shovels, etc., for CONVICTS; purse with money; locket; handfull of flowers; little satin slipper; diary-book; watch.

TIME IN REPRESENTATION—TWO HOURS AND A HALF.

[*For Synopsis and Stage Directions, see pag s 48, 49, and 50.*]

NOT GUILTY.

ACT I.

SCENE I.—*Southampton Bar.*

TRUMBLE *writing at an old-fashioned bureau covered with papers.*

WATTLES (C., *after pinning on ribbons*). There. a man needn't be born a seventh son to prophesy your future career. You've commander-in-chief written in every line of your noble, and intelligent physiognomy! (OMNES *laugh*.)

RECRUIT (*laughing stupidly*). Non, you bean't serious. sergeant?

WAT. Not serious! (*to* BYSTANDERS). Ladies and gentlemen, let me call your attention to this beautiful picture. Increase the nose, enlarge the forehead, bring out the chin, and change the entire expression of the countenance, and may I never taste ale again, but we've a living, breathing likeness of (*pointing to sign*) the Great Duke himself. (*laugh*) This other bow on your breast—your manly breast, and you'd be an ornament to——

Enter TRIGGS, *from house* R. *who is dressed in shabby black, and has the appearance of a lawyer's clerk.*

TRIGGS. A poulterer's shop! If you could only put your liver under one arm. and your gizzard under the other, I shouldn't know you from a prize turkey at Christmas. (*laugh*.)

WAT. (*turning to* TRIGGS). And you, my noble youth?

TRIG. No, don't—please don't. I've no pretension to anything of the kind; there isn't the slightest mystery concerning either of my parents, and I haven't such a thing as a strawberry mark anywhere about me.

WAT. You'll take the Queen's money?

TRIG. Not if I know it! I wouldn't rob her of a farthing.

WAT. A young fellow like you should serve your country.

TRIG. So I do—that is, I *serve* my countrymen. I'm a lawyer's clerk.

WATTLES *turns away in disgust and joins recruits, etc., about door, while* POLLY DOBBS *comes forward.* RECRUITS *and* SOLDIERS *gradually enter house,* L., SERGEANT *and* DRUMMER *remain.*

POLLY (*with affected surprise*). You here still, Mr. Triggs?

TRIG. *Mister* Triggs! Call me Joe—I can dispense with respect till we're married.

POL. Well, what nonsense you do talk, Joe; when you know I'm en-

gaged to go to India with Mrs. Doctor McTavish, and before many hours
are over shall be a-tossing on the briny ocean.

TRIG.—With those wavy outlines—oh!

POL. I've just taken leave of uncle, and my boxes are already on
board. A gi l must better herself, Joe.

TRIG. Better her elf! Haven't I fil'd my declaration and made you
a legal offer of marriage—before witnesses, mind you—before witnesses?

POL. (*contemptuously*). Marriage on seventy pounds a-year!

TRIG. With prospects, Miss Dobbs—with prospects!

POL. Most people who live in garrets have lots of those—acres of
tiles, and forests of chimney-pots!

TRIG Oh. don't turn up your delicious little snub at seventy pounds
a-year! Economically managed, it's a fortune.

POL Economically managed? Do I look like economy?

TRIG. Fat and feelings shoul always go together.

POL. Nonsense! the husband that I choose must be like a snail in one
thing—he must bring me a house on his back. (*with change of manner and
extending hand*) Good-bye, Joe ; this is about the forty-fifth parting we
have had during the last twenty-four hours. Good-bye, I shall come
back again. [POLLY *exits into house,* L.

TRIG. (*with emotion. and dropping her hand*). Come back! of course you
will—thin, perhaps, and wife to a Nabob, and mother to half-a-dozen
india-rubber looking children. (*looking after her*) Oh, woman, woman!
once it was love, and now it's furniture. But I'm a neglecting business,
though love is so much a matter of business now-a-days that it's difficult
to know one from the other. (*looking up at window of house,* L) There's
Trumble, hard at work at the quarterly accounts, twisting noughts into
sixes and nines—topping and tailing, he calls it. I was to be back in
twenty minutes with Mr. St. Clair, but, bless me—what can time matter
to old Trumble, except to charge for it? (SOLDIERS *singing within tavern
as* TRIGGS *exits,* R. U. E. TRUMBLE *rises from chair, comes to window.*)

TRUMBLE (*irritated, aside, and gnawing feather of pen*). Calculation's
impossible with all this noise. (*glancing out as* SOLDIERS. &c., *come down
stage ;* POLLY *also re-appears. talking to inn-keeper*) Gallant fellows—
they're to be shipped off in a few hours, and it's a consolation to think
we mayn't see any more of them.

RECRUITS *and* SOLDIERS *sit at table. Goes back to bureau and re-seats himself, as* ROBERT ARNOLD, *in the costume of a journeyman locksmith, enters
at back,* R, *as turning the corner of tavern. He carries a basket of tools at
his back, and is whistling merrily. Re-enter* POLLY, *from house,* L.

ROBERT. Hilloh. sergeant! Hilloh, Polly! (*seizing her round the
waist, gives her a kiss before she can prevent him*) If you will put such
tempting cherries in a hungry fellow's way you must expect he'll have
a snap at them. Don't pout, Polly, or I'll repeat the offence out of des-
peration. Let's have more beer—once ms more! I stand glasses round.
(*a l shout and come forward*) And Polly—(*stopping her as she is going*) touch
the rim of my glass with your lips, just to correct the acidity.

POL. (*laughing and shaking herself loose*) You'd be all the better for
correction of some kind. (*pretends to box his ear, then enters house,* L)

WAT. A parting glass, eh, B b!

ROB. Parting g'ass ? not a bit of it—I go with you.

ALL You! You go to the Injies—you!

ROB. (*laughing and striking attitude*). No less a person than Robert
Arnold! Bob Arnold on week days, and Mister Robert Arnold when he
walks out on a Sunday.

WAT. (*shaking hands*). I'm delighted! (MEN *shout "bravo"*) We're all delighted!

ROB. All but the women. (*chucking* POLLY *under chin as she pours out ale which she has brought*) Bless their little hearts, 'tisn't my fault if they love me.

POL. (*clapping hands*). We shall be fellow-passengers, then. Oh, how nice! [RECRUITS *exit into inn*, L.

ROB. Yes. (*placing basket of tools on stage by table*) There are my tools which I have used to-day for the last time, to take up the trade of war, and Mister Ormond Willoughby——

WAT. Our Captain!

ROB. Takes me out with him as confidential clerk, and (*laughs*) to reflect a lustre on the British army. (*oud laugh in house*, L. *They go up stage laughing and talking.* TRUMBLE *rises, places papers in bureau, which he locks, then re-appears at window.*)

TRUM. That fellow, Triggs, has loitered on the road as usual. I'd better meet Mr. St. Clair half way, for this noise is unendurable.

Shuts window, as he does so, SILAS JARRETT *appears at back, from* L. *Loud laugh in tavern as he enters. He pauses at sight of group before the tavern, and surveys the scene. He is a ragged young fellow with a sort of hybrid appearance, between a mendicant tramp and a dock laborer. A taste for gaudy colors is shown in the greasy red and yellow handkerchief twined about his neck, and the equally greasy ribbon that dangles from his torn straw hat. His hair, which is uncombed, hangs in tangled masses over his forehead, a sort of thatch, beneath which his eyes peer out in a sinister and savage manner.*

SILAS Curse them! what a row they're making! If I knew how to stop their merriment, I would! I can't bear to see people enjoying themselves; it's an insult to my rags and misery. (*still unperceived by the joyous group about tavern door, he comes slowly forward, limping slightly, as footsore*) Enjoy themselves! the fools! it's brief pleasure without money! There's Robert Arnold, honest, hardworking Robert—who's always mocking me, or patronizing me with the insolence of his pity. (*savagely*) Honest Robert! good Robert! hardworking Robert! Ah! if hate could kill you'd have been dead long ago. (*leans against wall of* TRUMBLE'S *house in the shadow, as* TRUMBLE *comes out, closes door behind him, and passing* SILAS *without notice, ext.* R. C.) There goes another sort of foo, a rich one, who plods! plods! plods! plods! like the working bee, not curing to enjoy the honey he creates. They're looking this way, and are talking about me no doubt. (*changing manner suddenly to that of a man laboring under semi-intoxication*) There's no mask like drunkenness, behind it one can learn the thoughts of others, and conceal one's own.

POL. (*speaking in group about tavern door*). Isn't that Silas Jarrett?

ROB. (*sitting on table*, C.) Drunk as usual.

POL. Why don't you get *him* to enlist, Sergeant Wattles?

WAT. Because I'm the only man from whom he won't take a shilling. By the way, have you ever remarked the singular likeness that exists between him and our young captain?

ROB. Who could be off remarking it. It's one of those freaks of Nature which Captain Ormond Willoughby has a right to complain of—that is, if he were aware of the existence of such an idle, quarrelsome vagabond.

WAT. How long has he been in Southampton?

POL. About a month, I think.

ROB. He landed from one of the French boats, and has been loafing in the docks ever since.

During the above conversation SILAS, *with a staggering step, has approached them. He tries to overhear what they are saying under cover of lighting his pipe, which he makes assumed drunken and ineffectual efforts to do.*

SIL. (*trying matches on sleeve*). Hang the matches! they won't take fire! That's because I m as damp outs de as I'm dry within. (*staggering as if by accident against* ROBERT) Hlloh! somebody's drunk here. (*hic*) Ha! it's you, Robert Arnold, it's you! (*hic*) Drunk as usual! I'm (*hic*) ashamed of you! (*all laugh*) Give me a light.

ROB. (*giving light*). Here's one; will you have anything else?

SIL. (*quickly*). Who's to pay? I haven't (*hic*) had the ghost of a farthing in my pocket for weeks; I've been going on tick like a clock, but (*hic*) I'm run down at last!

ROB. (*as* POLLY *fills glass and* SILAS *eagerly drinks*). I stand treat! (*giving* POLLY *money.*)

SIL. You seem flush of money just now. I shouldn't wonder but you could tell me what the taste of meat is like? I've quite forgotten.

ROB. Why don't you work?

SIL. (*with a drunken laugh*). Working! (*holding out hand which is shaking visibly*) Who do you think will engage a hand like that? Why (*hic*) it's more unsteady than my feet. I live like a dog and shall die like a dog.

ROB. There's my last half-crown, Silas. (*gives money*) But the captain's promised me an advance on my salary to-morrow.

SIL. (*who has clutched the half-crown*). The captain! What do you mean? I didn't (*hic*) know there was a captain of locksmiths.

ROB. (*laughs*). Locksmith! I screwed the last lock I ever intend to make, on a door, a couple of hours ago. After to-day I belong to the British army! (*putting his arm round a girl's waist.*)

Re-enter RECRUITS *and* SOLDIERS, L.

Lead the way, sergeant! We're going round the town for a spurt. We've light hearts, and (*slapping trousers*) empty pockets!

The DRUMMER *and* FIFER *who are now very drunk and unsteady, lead the way;* WATTLES, ROBERT, *and all the rest, except* POLLY *and* SILAS, *go off singing "The British Grenadiers."* POLLY *re-enters tavern, closing door in* SILAS' *face.* SILAS *comes down stage with an utter change of manner—steady as a rock, and with a face of fox-like cruelty and cunning. Night has been slowly drawing on.*

SIL. (*tossing coin in his hand*). What's half a crown to a man who has shaken a dice-box and cut cards with lords? Who has ridden in Rotten Row, and in the Bois de Boulogne, dined at the London Clubs, and swallowed ices at Tortoni's? I's something though, to a hunted and hungry devil just escaped from the hell of a French prison to suffer worse punishment—poverty in England! ugh! I know no deeper hell than that! (*as he is about to pocket half-crown,* MARGARET ARMITAGE *poorly and thinly clad in widow's weeds, enters L. C., hurriedly and laboring under strong nervous excitement. It is now night.*)

MARGARET (*aside, as catching the last word*). Who spoke of poverty? Surely he who speaks of that should feel for me! (*as urged by a desperate impulse, she lays her hand upon* SILAS' *arm*) Sir! oh, sir!

SIL. (*starting back*). Who are you? what do you want?

MAR. A poor widow, sir, without bread, and without a halfpenny to purchase any, through the life of my child——(*she stops, and her voice breaks into a sob.*)

SIL. Your child! Oh! you've a child then? It's an old story—but I like to have it complete. A baby, I suppose; "a little fair-haired, blue-eyed thing," they're always fair-haired and blue-eyed, the children of the poor!

MAR. A girl, six years old, and—starving!

SIL (*with a coarse laugh*). Six years old! Why doesn't she work?

MAR. Work! she is dying with hunger! and the fever that—— (*laying her hand on his sleeve.*)

SIL. (*shaking her roughly off*). Fever! Touch me again and I'll give you in charge. (*aside as he exits*) Fever! Life's worth something though one has only a half-crown's lease of it. (*enters tavern, L., slamming door behind him*)

MAR. (*endeavoring to follow him*). Oh, sir! in mercy! not for me—but for her! (*raising her hand with a gesture of despair as the tavern door swings to*) My child! my child! Heaven give me strength to crawl home and die beside her! It's all I dare pray for now! (*she again totters a few paces, supporting herself by wall, then sinks with a low cry on seat by table.* ROBERT ARNOLD *is heard singing off* L.)

ROBERT (*entering gayly, and slightly exhilarated by drink*).

> Now fare-thee-well, my own true love!
> A long farewell from me,
> I go to fight my country's foes—
> Far, far beyond the sea!   ·

My own true love! (*he laughs*) It wouldn't be easy to give her a name! not that I'm blind to the attractions of the sex. Bless it! but it's the difficulty of selection that has been my safe-guard. The candidates are all so beautiful! (*going to tavern*) Now to fetch my basket of tools—I've promised them to a shopmate as a legacy if—— (*while he is speaking* MARGARET *has half arisen, but sinks down again with a groan*) Hilloh! what was that? (*turning and seeing* MARGARET *in the shadow, as she is again striving to rise*) A woman! (*raises her a little*) What's the matter? are you ill? Lean on me! I'm not quite so steady as I should be, but lean on me. There! so, all right now! we're firm as a rock! as a couple of rocks! (*he has supported her towards door, recognizes her*) Mrs. Armitage!

MAR. (*faintly*). Robert Arnold!

ROB. What's the matter? you are crying! What do you want?

MAR. Bread!

ROB. Bread?

MAR. Not for myself, but for Alice—bread for my child!

ROB. Bread! bread! oh! brute, beast that I was, lodging in the same house, yet never to have guessed it! I knew that you were poor, very poor! but I never knew it had come to this pass—never!

MAR. Help me, Robert, Alice is starving!

ROB. (*now thoroughly sobered*). And I without a penny—my last money gone to that idle, skulking, ne'er-do-well Silas Jarrett. (*feeling hastily in pockets*) Not a penny! not one! not one!

MAR. (*very faintly*) Take me home! only take me home! oh! Robert, I must see my child before I die!

ROB. (*with forced gayety*). Die! nonsense! don't talk like that; we are close to the door of your house! You go up-stairs to Alice, and—and console her till I come. Oh! never fear but I'll come! I've no money, but I've friends, heaps of friends, crowds of friends! oceans of friends! (*speaking aside as he leads her off*, c) But how to find one at this time of night, I don't know! (*gayly as her head droops on his shoulder*) Tell Alice, dear little Alice! that Robert won't be five minutes! she shall have bread, bread and meat, and plenty of it! plenty, plenty of it! (*aside, with a gasp as overcoming his emotion*) Damme! if I have to go down on my knees and beg for it in the streets she shall have it!

[*They exeunt*, ROBERT *half carrying* MARGARET.

As they disappear, SILAS JARRETT *re-appears from tavern.*

SILAS (*wiping mouth*). That beggar woman's gone, I see! She gave me quite a turn—first by laying her hand so suddenly on my arm, and then by talking about fever. Since I escaped from that cursed prison I'm nervous at my own shadow. There's, ah! India's the place for me! where a horsekeeper may become a prince, or at least a prince's prime minister, if he has his wits about him. (*he shivers and draws his ragged coat about him*) Not like in this foggy climate, where at every step you're asked for a certificate of character. I'd work my passage anywhere so I could get out of this place, but with every ship it's the same result—one glance at these rags, and "kick him overboard," roars the captain. (*he kicks out his leg as he says this, and strikes his foot against the basket of tools, which* ROBERT *has placed by seat at table*) What's this? a basket (*taking it up*) of tools! locksmith's tools! It must be Arnold's! a hammer, a file, a screwdriver, pincers, and keys, and no end of keys, and a bunch of skeletons! (*holding up skeleton keys, with a chuckling laugh*) I should know their utility—the crooked little darlings! each one looks like a note of interrogation! an "inquire within" that's sure to be profitably answered, ha, ha! I always welcome old friends! Somebody's coming! more passengers for the Madras boat! I'll place these tools in a safe place. (*laughs*) Where their owner won't find them in a hurry.

Slinks off at back, keeping in the shadow, as MR. ST. CLAIR *and* TRUMBLE *enter* R. C.—ST. CLAIR *is dressed as for a voyage, he carries a small valise.*

TRUMBLE. But, my dear sir, my very dear sir, as a man, I may approve your motive; but as a lawyer——
CLAIR (*laughing, and placing his hand on* TRUMBLE'S *shoulder*). My dear Trumble, sink the lawyer in the man!
TRUM. Impossible! do that, and what becomes of the law courts? What you propose, Mr. St. Clair, is to sacrifice at least one-third of your fortune.
CLAIR. The whole business is one of simple justice. My uncle's death has left me master of an ample fortune—a portion of which is gained from an estate in India to which our family has no right in equity.
TRUM. But in law? your uncle gained the cause
CLAIR. Unjustly, as I'm most reluctantly compelled to believe. It's then for me, as my uncle's inheritor, to make restitution to Mr. Armitage.
TRUM. He died in India——
CLAIR. Very poor! leaving a widow, as I understand, and a daughter in England. My voyage to Madras is, as you know, to attend the bedside of my sick mother. Spare no pains in my absence to trace out the surviving members of the Armitage family. The re-assignment you already have, and this case, which I have just received from my agent, contains a sum sufficient to meet their possible necessities till my return.

TRUM. Will you come up into the office while I write out an acknow-ledgment?

CLAIR. I'll wait for you here. We won't say good-bye till the last bell rings.

SILAS JARRETT, *who has again appeared at back just as* ST. CLAIR *passes the leather note-case to* TRUMBLE, *starts as he hears the latter mention the money it contains—he creeps nearer, keeping within the shadow of wall, then crouches down close to ground, the head raised, the neck outstretched, listening.*

TRUM. (*with hearty burst of emotion*). You're a good fellow, St. Clair, and were there many like you, you'd be the ruin of our profession, that's all I know.

He crosses over to house, opens door with latch-key, enters, and closes it behind him. ST. CLAIR, *down stage, lights cigar.* SILAS JARRETT, *who al-most seems to have changed his body as well as his manner, creeps down the stage with all the lithe quickness and silence of the snake, till he commands a view of the first floor window, through which* TRUMBLE *is seen to enter room with light. He opens bureau, closes it, re-locks it, and then disap-pears,* SILAS, *who has gradually raised himself first to his knees, then to his feet, retreats again into shadow, and glides off, rapidly, with a gesture of triumph, as* ST. CLAIR, *turning, goes slowly up stage.*

CLAIR. Jolly old boy, Trumble! With a rough outside, he's full of the milk of human kindness.

Enter ROBERT ARNOLD, *in great agitation, hastily,* R.

ROBERT. I beg your pardon, but just one word, if you please. (*he makes a movement as to place his hand on* ST. CLAIR'S *arm, the latter draws back*)

CLAIR. Who are you, fellow?

ROB. Oh! don't be afraid, sir! There's nothing wrong about me. My name's Arnold—Robert Arnold, locksmith—leastways, I was a lock-smith a few hours ago, but I shall be a soldier when——

CLAIR (*impatiently*). What's all this to me? What do you want?

ROB. (*abruptly*). Charity!

CLAIR (*stepping still further back*). A beggar!

ROB. (*drawing himself up with a momentary pride which he suppresses*). I! a beggar! Well, I suppose I'm something of the kind—though, heaven be thanked, I've never had need to ask help of anybody for myself, and if I hadn't been scattering my money all day like a fool, I shouldn't now be begging for another.

CLAIR. What other?

ROB. A poor woman, sir, starving! and her child, too! An angel of six years old! Dying! dying! sir! for want of that which a few pence could purchase!

CLAIR. Can this be true?

ROB. True! I left her but just now, praying her to take heart and wait for my return; I rushed off to my employer, woke him up by throwing a stone through his window, and asked him for a loan, but the granite-hearted old hunks, knowing that I leave Southampton at day-break, cursed me for a drunken rogue—*me!* Robert Arnold! and slam-med down his window—I tried elsewhere with like success. Don't go, sir, don't go. Beggar! (*snatching off cap, and holding it out*) Yes, sir, I am begging! and when I think of her and her child's suffering, I'm not ashamed of it!

CLAIR (*hesitating*). But——

ROB. Bring it home to yourself, sir; suppose that *you* had a child, or a mother——

CLAIR (*with emotion and speaking hastily as the door of* TRUMBLE'S *house is heard to open, and* TRUMBLE *com s out*). Hush! take this! (*giving a crumpled paper*) I *have* a mother—a sick mother. Let those whom this m ney relieves, pray that s e may live to look once more upon the face of her son. (*aside, as he crosses to* TRUMBLE) Not a word of this to Trumble, or he ll lecture me again. (*he takes* TRUMBLE'S *arm, and they exeunt hurriedly.*)

ROB. (*who has unfolded paper*). A five pound note! (*cuts a caper*) There'll be more than one joyful heart to-night in Southampton. (*cutting another caper*) I'll buy Alice a doll!

As he runs off, R., SILAS JARRETT *creeps on with a rapid crouching step, he carries, hugged up, half concealed by his rags,* ROBERT'S *basket of tools; he opens door with a skeleton key, enters stealthily, closing it again silently, is seen to open bureau, with the skeleton keys from* ROBERT'S *bag, and to take out papers, he closes the bureau, leaves the room.*

The Scene changes to

SCENE II.—*Interior of a Garret, miserably furnished.*

Enter MARGARET, *with candle and jug of water, door,* R.

MARGARET (*in accents of terror, leaning over child*). Alice, Alice! my own darling! My dear. dear lit le girl! speak to me! only lo k at me! Ah! (*with a cry*) not a word, not a glance! (*starting to her feet*) She is dying! And yet Robert Arno d told me to wait and hope! Oh, what shall I do? what st all I do? Not a breath, not a movement! Tears and kisses, all—all are alike useless! (*her tone changes to one of strong bitterness*) And why should I wish to call her back? Why should life exist, when hope is dead? Enough of suff ring! I cannot fight the battle of life al ne! (*she falls across bed fainting, as* ALICE, *raising herself slightly, speaks in a faint voice.*)

ALICE. Mamma, mamma! (*frightened, and placing her hand on* MARGA-RET'S *head*) Oh, my dear mamma!

MAR. (*with a cry rises to her feet, and looking vaguely round, takes several steps as one in a dream*). Yes, dear! I cannot see you, but I hear your voice. Alice!

She makes a step or two forward from the bed, then, with another low, moaning cry, falls on face, there is a momentary stillness, followed by a loud knocking at door, and ROBERT ARNOLD *calls from outside,* R.

ROBERT. Open the door, open the door, Mrs. Armitage! it is I—I, Robert Arnold! I bring you help! What was that cry—that noise? Open, or——

The door is burst open, and ROBERT *enters precipitately on scene, carrying a basket of provisions, which he places on the table, then recoils aghast as he sees* MARGARET *stretched on the ground—bending over her.*

Ah, miserable woman! what have you done? She's only fainted, thank Heaven!

MAR. (*repulsing him*). Not me—not me—my child is dead. It is I who have killed her—I have killed my child!

ROB. (*rushing to bed, and taking* ALICE *in his arms*). No, no—she still breathes! It is this stifling atmosphere that is killing her!

MAR. There is more air in the next room. Carry her there! quick! quick!

ROB. Heaven be praised—we shall save her yet!

[*They exeunt,* L., *into the inner garret.*

As they do so, a confusion of voices is heard in the street below—" Stop thief! stop thief!" *etc., etc., and* SILAS JARRETT, *panting and out of breath, dashes into the room,* R., *the bunch of skeleton keys still in his hand, and the leather case, which he holds, tight to his breast.*

SIL. The door below being open, I took the liberty of entering without knocking. Where am I? (SILAS. *who has approached the half-glazed door,* L., *recoils*) Robert Arnold! (*he re-crosses stage to door, but again recoils, as voices are heard, and confusion, as of several persons ascending stairs.*)

VOICES. It was this house! I saw him enter! Keep the door fast below!

SIL. They're mounting the staircase—ah, the chimney! In a minute I'm on the roof, but first of all I return, with many thanks, your bunch of keys, Mr. Robert Arnold—(*throwing them down on table*) and with them this pocket-book. (*while speaking he has taken out the contents and crammed the notes and papers into his pockets*) If I can but get down to the Docks before the boat starts, I have once more my foot upon the ladder of fortune. (*throws pocket-book on the floor*) I leave you a ten-pound note. It's a parting gift, honest Robert, but I doubt if you'll thrive with it. (*disappears with a laugh behind the counterpane which conceals fireplace. As it drops behind him, several persons, with* TRUMBLE *and two* POLICEMEN, *enter room hastily,* R. *door. One of the* POLICEMEN *carries* ROBERT'S *basket of tools.*)

TRUM. (*to* POLICEMAN). You're sure the man entered this house?

FIRST POLICE. Quite!

TRUM. You didn't see his face?

FIRST POL. No, he rushed by me with his head down as I opened the door of the office. I would have caught him, but I tumbled over this basket which he had left in his haste.

TRUM. (*taking it*). A basket of workman's tools!

ROB. (*entering from room,* L.). Workman's tools—they are mine! (*general movement.*)

ALL. Yours!

ROB. Who brought them here? and what's the meaning of all this?

FIRST POL. (*taking some things from table and holding them up triumphantly*). A bunch of skeleton keys

ROB. They're mine, also,

TRUM. The same, I've no doubt, that were used to force my bureau.

ROB. (*turning sharply upon him*). What's that? What the devil do you mean? (*looking angrily around*) Do any of you dare to suspect——

A MAN (*who looks a working baker, pushing forward*). Stop a moment—I can settle all this: That's the man who a few minutes ago rushed into my shop as I was just putting up the shutters and wanted to change a five-pound note to buy a quartern loaf!

TRUM. (*to* ROBERT) Where did you steal that note from?

ROB. Steal? It was given to me in the street to save this poor woman and her child. (*pointing to* MARGARET, *who, entering from the inner gar-*

ret, L., *stands petrified by the scene before her, the two* POLICEMEN *having quietly moved, one on each side of* ROBERT.)

MAR. It is true, gentlemen; it is true.

FIRST POL. (*picking up leather case from floor*). Whose is this letter case?

ROB. (*indignantly*). How should I know?

TRUM. It's mine—the one just taken from my bureau. (*opening it*) It still contains a note marked on the back " Edward St. Clair."

BAKER. That was the name on the back of that note he offered me.

TRUM. (*to* ROBERT). What have you done with the rest of the money?

ROB. (*aghast*) Done! (*quite bewildered*) I don't know what you mean.

TRUM (*to* POLICEMEN). I charge that man with theft!

ROB. Me!

MAR. Robert Arnold! Robert Arnold is incapable of such an act——

TRUM. Let him explain how this letter case, containing money and papers, which has just been stolen from my office, came into his hands? one of the notes it contained having already been offered for change by him!

MAR. By him!

TRUM. But a few minutes ago, and let him also explain how his basket of tools came to be by my broken bureau?

FIRST POL. Minus this bunch of skeletons which I found on the table here! (*one of the* POLICEMEN *slips handcuffs on* ROBERT, *while the other places his hand on his shoulder.*)

ROB. I am not guilty! not guilty, on my word! (MARGARET *utters a cry of horror—Tableau, and closed in.*)

SCENE III.—*A portion of the Southampton Docks. Steamer bell ringing.*

TRIGGS *enters greatly excited,* L. *He has a bunch of ribbons fastened to his tall napless hat.*

TRIGGS (*sings*). " Solomon Lobb he lost his nob,
                And all for love and glory." (*stops abruptly.*)
I've done it! I've been and gone and done it! I've taken the shilling—the fatal shilling! and Polly and I sail in the same ship, and we'll have our game of pitch and toss together! I couldn't stand the idea of that nabob, and the India rubber accessories. (*bell ceases—stopping* PORTER, *who enters,* L., *with portmanteau on shoulder*) What's that bell?

PORTER. The Madras boat just started.

TRIGGS. What's the Madras boat to do with me? I belong to the troop ship—you may possibly have perceived a military air about me?

POR. Well, you look like a sort o' Johnny Raw; but clear the way, please, here's more luggage coming. (*exit* R., *as more* PORTERS *come on* L. —TRIGGS *stops their trucks, and insists, fussily, on reading the addresses.*)

TRIGGS Now, my good men, my good men! you may possibly be unaware that I form part of the British army—respect the defenders of your country, respect the—— (*reads address*) "Mrs. Turmeric," Mrs. Turmeric may pass. Captain Ormond Willoughby—ah! we belong to the same regiment—fellow soldiers, fellow soldiers. Ah! this is what I want, Mrs. McTavish! here we have it. ' Miss Dobbs," Miss Mary Dobbs, one trunk and four band-boxes—quite correct! (*after making a memorandum*) My luggage. (*placing a very small brown paper parcel with much solemnity on top of luggage*) My luggage, it goes with hers. (*turning to side as* PORTERS, *highly irritated, wheel off truck,* R.) Here she comes! wrapped up in me and other comforters!

POLLY *enters, hurriedly,* L., *enveloped in cloak and many mufflers, as for a voyage—she tripps across stage, but pauses in* C *, without seeing* TRIGGS.

POLLY. I've been looking everywhere for Joe Triggs, I thought at least he would have seen me down to the boat. Poor Joe! I never knew I liked him so much till now I'm about to leave him—ah! (*screams as* TRIGGS, *who comes down stage, throws his arms about her*) You've given me quite a turn!

TRIGGS. In the right direction, I hope. Having issued an attachment, I take the body!

POLLY (*bridling*). You'll take yourself off, Mr. Triggs, such conduct at parting, too!

TRIGGS. Parting! (*shows ribbons on hat*) Permit me to call your attention to this—the last new article in ribbons.

POLLY (*with a little scream*). Why, Joe, you don't mean to say you've 'listed?

TRIGGS (*sings*). " My boat is on the shore. and my bark is on the sea." And I sail from Albion's shore, with thee, Miss Dobbs, with thee! I couldn't stand that idea about the nabob. Wattles tossed up the shilling, and woman won! Don't speak! I know what I have sacrificed—I might have been Lord Chancellor, but I gave Trumble the *sack* in preference to sitting upon it myself.

POLLY. Mr. Trumble! oh! haven't you heard the news, Joe?

TRIGGS. What news?

POLLY. Robert Arnold has been taken up for robbing the office! Mr. Trumble's office!

TRIGGS. Robert Arnold! Oh, come now, that won't do!

POLLY. The money's been found upon him, and——

TRIGGS. I don't believe it! I won't believe it! (*he walks about stage, pounding hat which he has taken off, till it is entirely out of shape*) Why I'd rather suspect myself!

POLLY. And so would I—much rather!

TRIGGS. It's a plot of some kind, or a case of mistaken identity. It's anything—everything, but the one thing, and that's the truth! Polly, dear! a man doesn't rub shoulders with the law as I've done for fifteen years, and not know the signs of a thief when he meets him. The first thing is to engage counsel; I know one, with a face like a warming-pan, and lungs like a blacksmith's bellows. It's more difficult, of course, when a chap's innocent, because he's not up to the thing, but we'll pull him through—we'll pull him through!

POLLY. You're a good fellow, Joe. Mind, we sail in an hour.
[*Exit,* R.

TRIGGS. In an hour! And Robert Arnold! What's to become of him? No notion of the law of evidence—a mere child—couldn't prove an alibi if he tried! and quite unaware, in a legal point of view, of the power of lungs and brass, but I'll sift the case, I'l—— (*moving to side he encounters* SERGEANT WATTLES. *stiff and stern, with several* SOLDIERS *and* RECRUITS *from* L) Ah! my dear Wattles!

WAT. (*with crushing dignity*). Your what?

TRIG. Wattles, I've a favor to ask of you; could we arrange it, that I come out by the next boat?

WAT. (*in a voice of thunder*). Fall in, sir, or we shall fall out!

TRIG. Haven't you got a heart, sergeant?

WAT. Yes, of oak.

TRIG. But that's no reason your head should be made of the same material; I want to do a friend a service.

WAT. Your services belong to the Queen.

TRIG. Of course they do; but I know her, bless her, she's a kind, good-hearted lady, and will stretch a point—besides, she'll have her shilling's worth out of me before long, having taken the money I shall not shirk the liability. I've a charac er to lose, sergeant.

WAT. Then take my advice, and lose it at once.

TRIG. You wouldn't advise that if you knew the trouble I've had to get it together. You know Robert Arnold ?

WAT. I know no hing but the captain's orders. Private friendships must give way to pab ic duty.

TRIG. But Robert Arnold——

WAT. Leave him to the law.

TRIG. That's a pretty sty.e of baby-farming; you haven't spent fifteen years in a lawyer's office.

WAT. Recruits on board ! R ght shoulder forward—march ! (SOLDIERS *gather about* TRIGGS, *and he is hustled off*, R., *vainly protesting.*)

SCENE IV.—*A portion of the deck and interior of a sleeping cabin on board the "Begum," packetship to Madras.*

SILAS (*listening*). All quiet ! Nothing but the pleasant lap of the water against the vessel's sides ! I've slipped down here to enjoy a glass in quiet. (*drinks*) Champagne ! champagne ! (*fills and laughs*) What a wine ! This is my second bottle, and I deserve it after my exertions (*pushing up wig, and discovering face*) How stifling hot this cabin is, and the more I drink, the more it increases my thirst. (*drinks*) Well, I can afford it—I can afford oceans of drink ! I can drink gold if I like. (*looks stealthily towards ladder at back, then draws out a packet of papers and notes, which he turns over greedily and hurriedly*) A fortune ! a fortune ! But what's this paper ! (*examining it*) " E lward St. Clair's assignment of estate in favor of "—Bah ! better burn all this ! (*he rises unsteadily, reaches at lamp, then fails back in chair*) D mn—the lamp ! or rather the lamps, for that con- founde l s ewa d must have lighted another—where's the bottle ? *clutching it after several ineffectual efforts*) The ship seems spinning round like a tee-tee- ee—(*hic*) tee-to-tum ! A storm brewing, I suppose ! Let it brew ! I'm rich enough to laugh at storms of every kind ! (*drinks from bottle*) Glorious wine ! I haven't tasted it for many a long day, but as the (*hic*) bird returns to its nest—so I (*hic*) return to the bottle ! (*drinks*) It's empty !

In replacing it on table, he knocks over glass which falls with a crash. In en- deavoring to save it he sweeps with his arms the notes and papers from table. At some time a pile of cloaks is thrust aside, and ST CLAIR *rises from one of the sofas beneath the berths, with angry impatience.*

CLAIR. Hilloh ! what are you making all this noise about ? (*sleepily approaching table and yawning*) If you can't sleep yourself don't deprive me of that privi ege.

SIL (*this greed overcoming in part—but in part only—his intoxication*). Stand b ck ! don't come a step nearer ! keep back ! I warn you ! (*he throws h mself upon his knees, clutching up the scattered notes and papers with the threaten ng grasp of a wild cat*)

CLAIR (*aside*). He's drun k. (*kind y*) Let me help you—I fell asleep before I could undress and get into my berth. I think I ought to thank you for waking me up. (*stooping to pick up one of the notes*) Do let me he p you.

SIL. (*crouching over and grasping notes*). Keep back—keep back--they belong to me ! If you touch them I'll call for help—I wi.l ! I will !

CLAIR (*laughing*). Oh, as you please; I don't wish to rob you.

SIL. (*on his knees, with a start*). Rob! what do you mean by that? (*rising to his feet*) Who spoke of robbery?

CLAIR (*same pleasant tone*). Not I. There, don't excite yourself. Here are some of your notes. and—(*about to hand paper. he glances at it, and starts*) My signature! (*stepping back as the other advances, and placing paper under lamp, holding* SILAS *back some time at arm's length*) The assignment I gave to Trumble! How came you by this?

SIL. It's mine! it's mine!

CLAIR (*casting him off as he endeavors to grasp paper*). That remains to be proved! (*snatching up note from table. And this note endorsed by me! It's for you to stand back, rascal! (*throwing him off as he makes a cat-like clutch at note.*)

SIL. (*hoarsely, and mad with excitement*). My money! (*he snatches up knife from table, but* ST. CLAIR, *drawing a pistol from pocket, stops him as he crouches to spring*)

CLAIR (*covers him with pistol, and extending the other hand, speaks with intense calmness*). Give me the remainder of those notes.

SIL. (*aghast*). Who are you?

CLAIR. Edward St. Clair! This paper bears my signature, and these notes are mine!

SIL. Give them back? Never!

CLAIR (*the same calm determination*). Then I summon the captain to judge between us.

SIL. (*as struck by a sudden thought*). Two can play at that game. Help —help! murder! thieves!

CLAIR. Rascal! (*he seizes him and thrusts him back over table, from which the bottles roll to floor. In the struggle* SILAS'S *wig and beard come off*) Ha!

SIL. (*half choking*). Help! murder!

During the struggle SAILORS *appear on deck, descend ladder, and enter cabin confusedly. They precipitate themselves on* ST. CLAIR, *drag him back, and wrest the pistol from his hand. Taking advantage of his release,* SILAS, *with the agility of a cat, springs up the ladder and appears on deck, as the* CAPTAIN *of the steamer approaches* ST. CLAIR.

CAPTAIN. What does all this mean?

CLAIR (*shaking himself loose from the* SAILORS' *grasp, and pointing to wig and beard on table*). It means that you have seized the wrong man, and are letting the thief escape!

Followed by the SAILORS, *he makes a rush to the ladder, but recoils as the cry of* "Man overboard! man overboard!" *resounds through the ship;* SILAS *having sprung up on the bulwarks, as the* MAN AT THE WHEEL *and others make a rush at him, stands for a moment, his figure illuminated by the moonlight; then, as their arms are stretched out to grasp him, with a laugh of defiance, takes a "header" into the sea. Act closes on tableau,* SAILORS *unslinging boat, etc., etc., with effective groupings above and below deck.*

CURTAIN.

ACT II.

SCENE.—*The Quarries at Dartmoor.*

Enter JACK SNIPE, *with* TWO CONVICTS, R., *also in "good conduct" dress, stops in his work, looks round to be sure that no warder is listening, then comes down the stage. Several* CONVICTS, *who have also stopped work, follow his example. At rising of curtain, the* CONVICTS *are all at work, some wheeling barrows from back and off,* L.

JACK (*as* CONVICTS *group about him*). How did I get the name of Jack-in-the-Box? H'ignoramuses! *consult* the hannals of your country. Ah! it was a caper! (*sings.*)

> When first I did start, with my eye on some mart,
>   Not caring for bruises or knocks,
> Like a nimble young boy, I jumped with much joy,
>   As I hit on my plan of the BOX.
>
> I'd a caution on top to " keep this side up,"
>   Addressed to the Liverpool Docks,
> And the Company's man, not knowing my plan,
>   Would forward ME pack'd in my box. (*all laugh.*)
>
> When landed on shore and put into store,
>   I'd creep round the place in my socks;
> If I found the coast clear and had nothing to fear,
>   What swag I cramm'd into that box.
>
> At last I was sold, like many of old,
>   By one I had helped in distress.
> I was taken and tried, and the judge did decide
>   For five years I should wear this gray dress.
>   (*all join in chorus.*)

> For five years he should wear this gray dress.

Enter SILAS JARRETT, *from back, wearing a warder's dress, appearing up among rocks.*

SIL. Skulking work, you rascals! If I hear that noise again I'll report every one of you.

JACK (*in a hurried whisper*). It's the new warder! he is a Tartar! (*they disperse and resume work as before—*JACK *works by* R. 1 *wing.*)

SIL. Is that you, Jack Snipe?

JACK. I wish it warn'! 'Appy and proud to make the situation over to somebody else.

SIL. How dare you answer me?

JACK (*with mock surprise*) You! I'm blessed if I knowed you afore! (*takes off cap with ironical humility*) You're the hemperor of all the Rooshias, you are! When my respect for myself becomes flabby, I'll come to you for starch.

SIL. Get to your work—and that other skulker there No 47! (*pointing to* ROBERT ARNOLD, L, *who, at the sound of his voice, has staggered to his feet, but without turning towards him*) I'll soon have him stripped of his

good conduct dress and put on the chain gang, if I see more of his idling.
[*Exit at back*, R.

JACK (*looking after him as he exits*). You're a cock as knows how to crow, you do! You ain't been here more than a week, but you've made yourself already a marked man among us—one as will have his comb cut afore-long. (*gets to work at* c. *of stage—watching* ROBERT ARNOLD, *who has re-commenced work, but after a few strokes of the pick, pauses utterly exhausted*) Hi.loh! No. 47 is a-workin' up for the sick dodge—not a bad dodge neither! (*the pick drops from* ROBERT'S *hand and he supports himself against a piece of rock.* JACK SNIPE, *a little up stage, watching him.*)

ROB. I can bear this fate no longer. Strength, hope, patience, every thing has deserted me—everything but despair. What dreary months have pass'd since that terrible condemnation, and yet the crowded court is always before my eyes, and the stern voice of the judge sounding in my ears! Merciful Heaven! what a fate for an innocent man! The very education my dear mother impoverished herself to give me, that I might make my way in the world, only increases the sense of degradation. To be condemned to seven years' companionship with men whose very aspect makes me tremble, better death in any form, so that it be swift and sure. (*his head droops upon his breast, but he raises it quickly as* JACK SNIPE *creeps up and slaps him on the shoulder.*)

JACK. Cheer up, 47! I never see a chap take on as you do. When things can't be mended, grin and bear 'em, that's the motter of yourn to command, Jack Snipe.

ROB. But *I* was innocent!

JACK (*with cheerful briskness*). Of course you is! There's not a chap in this 'ere delightful com-munity as doesn't say the same, on'y he's speaking his *conviction*.

ROB. I swear to you——

JACK (*stopping him and looking hastily round*). Don't! that is, don't do it in that solemn manner. Some o' these fellers might take it into their heads to bel eve you.

ROB. Well!

JACK. And you'd lose their respect. that's all!

ROB (*turning away with a gesture of despair*). Into what an abyss have I fallen!

JACK (*aside, with rapid change of manner*). He's a-cryin'! (*again looking round cautiously, he comes c.ose to* ROBERT, *and touches him on the arm*) I say, stow that! If I've said anything as cuts ag'in the grain, I'm sorry for it. (*very kindly*) Oh! never mind me! give 'em vent! I've paid the water rates too often myself to cut 'em off from anybody else, besides, I've taken a l king to you, No. 47, you're so like a brother of mine.

ROB. Indeed!

JACK (*quickly*). He wasn't one o' my sort, mind yer, but a soldier as died out in the Injies; had he lived, p'raps I shouldn't be here—I wasn't born a thief.

ROB. No man is——

JACK. No, but he's born with a happetite, and some are born with big 'uns. without any means of satisfyin' 'em. It's all very well for people to talk about the 'ead and the 'art, but the stummick, the stummick's the wulnerable part of man's anatomy.

ROB. (*carelessly*). So your brother's death made you a thief?

JACK. He died a-fightin' the battles of his country, and his wife, who'd followed him ha'f round *this* world when he was alive, thought it her dooty, poor thing! to follow him into t'other, and there was a l.ttle kid left for me to purwide for.

Rob. A heavy responsibility!

Jack. It were. Bless its 'art! it *was* a baby! Give it an oyster shell or an old stocking to suck, and it 'ud be happy for hours. It nestled in my arms the first time it saw me, and if I hadn't lain upon it now and then acciden'ally, I don't think it would have cried much!

Rob. Surely you might have supported it honestly?

Jack (*with sudden fierceness*). I worked day and night, but it wasn't no good, 'twasn't often I cou'd take the little 'un's hammock by surprise, and astonish it with a lining. T'ade w s bad, and I got out of collar. There's two roads— he right 'un and the wrong 'un. The right 'un got shut up, and the kid—(*his voice grows husky and he wipes his eyes*) 'twasn't half as high as this pick, got ill—I took the wrong road, and the wrong road brought me here. (*as if ashamed of his emotion he turns away, and commences working with his pick, singing, with a sort of bravado*)

I'd a caution on top to keep this side up,
Addres ed to the Liverpool Dock.

Rob. And the child?

Jack (*dropping pick, and turning towards him, his eyes full of tears*). You won't chaff m', No 47? But to see that boy again I'd let 'em chop t ese two hands off!

Rob. (*very kindly*). Poor fellow!

Jack (*speaking rapidly*). I know the streets—know 'em well, mind ye! And when I think of a bit of a baby a-picking up its livin' like a houseless dog in the gut ers, it's a wonder I don't break out or do something desprit! It's the devil's cunning agin a child's i..nocence! You wouldn't offer odds on the child, No. 47, would you?

Rob. I feel for you.

Jack (*recovering his brisk manner*). Thank ye. Then kindness for kindness, (*lowering voice*) it's a friend us gives you the office—be on your guard, No. 47!

Rob. Of what?

Jack. O. the new warder, him as was app'inted last week—you two have met 'fore?

Rob. We have—often. How he comes here is another mystery I cannot so ve.

Jack. Well, there isn't much love lost atween you! Chut, here he comes, and with that creepin' creature as we calls the Polecat. I'd give some hin' to know what them two are conversin' about.

They both resume work as Silas Jarrett *re-appears at back from* R., *accompanied by the* Polecat, *a mean, cadaverous looking convict in " good conduct " dress.*

Silas (*in low voice to the* Polecat, *as they come down stage*). You're quite sure of what you say?

Pole (*in a low piping voice, interrupted by cough*). Yes, yes, the plan of es ape is all arranged—No. 50, that's old Isaac Vidler, you know him as we calls the " Patriarc ," takes the lead and gives the signal. The warders are to be overpowered, and then each man makes a run for it.

Jack (R, *striving to hear*). What is that sneakin' creatur' saying?

Sil. This wil get you a free pardon (*aside, as he moves down stage*) and me increased confidence. It was a great thought of mine to come here. When the wolves are on your track there's no place of safety like the lion's den! It's better to be the guardian of the cage, than to be shut up in it one's self Had I only secured the money and papers before I leaped from the deck of that cursed boat, I might have put myself beyond the possibility of pursuit. Now I have work d my way here to watch over my friend Robert Arnold—while he's in England there's no real safety for me! Fear and hate (*he is glancing furtively towards* ARNOLD *as he speaks*) are both powerful agents, but when *combined* they are irresistible!

The POLECAT, *who from nature is always sneaking about, comes face to face with* JACK SNIPE, *unexpected by the latter, who is trying to listen*—JACK *immediately resumes work with superfluous energy.*

JACK. (*hammering at slate and singing*)

> When landed on shore and put into store
> I'd creep round the place in my socks!

POLECAT (*with quick movement back to* SILAS). We're watched! (*coughs as usual behind his hand*)

SIL. (*angrily to* JACK). How dare you sing? 'Tis against regulations!

JACK (R.). Is it? Well if I don't conform to the rules of the establishment, you can dismiss me—I ain't attached to the situation.

SIL. (*to* ARNOLD, *who has paused in his work and turned towards them*). I'll report you both (*cro ses to* L.) and you, too, No. 47.

ROB. I hear, but refuse to exchange words with you, Silas Jarrett.

SIL. (*raising small cane he carries*). Take care! (JACK *moves to* C., *and works so as to be at the elbow of* SILAS *for his next turn*)

ROB. (*throwing aside pick, and folding arms*). Of what—of you? (SILAS *lowers cane and draws back*) I can't fear what I despise.

SIL. (*laughs, but lowers cane*). The contempt of a felon. (ARNOLD *turns away*) When we last met in Southampton I didn't think to see you in this interesting costume, No. 47.

JACK (*who has again sidled up*). Well, they don't seem the right sort of togs for him, do they, guv'nor? while (*glancing meaningly over* SILAS) to some I know they'd come nat'ral—like their own skins, in fact.

SIL. (*turning upon him*). What do you mean?

JACK. Nothing my means are limited!

SIL. Now I give you fair warning.

JACK. Wish you would give me warning—I'd take it and go! (*aside*) Oh, he's enough to make a bed-post savage!

WARDER (*who enters hastily, addressing* SILAS). Get your fellows together. The governor is showing some visitors over the quarries.

SILAS *gets back of* JACK, *who is at work*—JACK *throws a shovel full of dust over his back. Several other* WARDERS *enter, all armed; the* CONVICTS, *good and bad conduct men—all form oblique line from* R. 1 E., *double file, and pass by flote to go off* C. *platform*—JACK *and* ROBERT *last—this must be timed as* ROBERT *gets close to* MARGARET *at recognition*—ARNOLD *and* JACK SNIPE *side by side. While this is going on, the* GOVERNOR *of the Prison descends by the road,* R. U. E., *conducting* ST. CLAIR, MARGARET, TRUMBLE *and several other* VISITORS, LADIES *and* GENTLEMEN, *to the prison.*

GOVER. (C.). These are the new workings, we have only lately been quarrying here—quite new ground.

MAR. (L., *aside, and clinging to* ST. CLAIR'S *arm, as some of the* CONVICTS, *sullen and scowling, slouch past and disappear, two and two, by middle road at back*) Surely poor Robert Arnold cannot be among these men—not among these!

ST. CLAIR (L. C., *also in aside*). Restrain all emotion, I beg of you.

Remember I am here to save—my return from India had no other ob-
ject! but in these places all must be done by rule!

TRUM. (L., *same tone*). A little patience—a little patience, that's all, my
dear lady!

MAR. (*shuddering and drawing back*). What dreadful faces! And that
fetter on the leg!

As she speaks ARNOLD *and* JACK SNIPE, *walking in double file across stage,
pass before her. At the sound of her voice the former starts, and moved
by sudden impulse, turns towards her.*

ARNOLD. Margaret!

MAR. Robert Arnold! (*she is springing forward, but is stopped by* ST.
CLAIR, *who draws her back with a gesture of caution*—ARNOLD *passes up and
off stage, as the* GOVERNOR, &c., *gather about* MARGARET.)

ST. CLAIR (*with a forced gayety*). This lady has lately risen from a sick
bed, and this strange scene has tried her nerves a little! (*aside to* MAR-
GARET) Pray be careful!

MAR. (*same tone as the* GOVERNOR, *and the party move up stage*). I must
speak to him!

CLAIR. Think of Alice, your daughter.

MAR I do think of her, St. Clair. and remember she owes her life to
Robert Arnold—I must speak to him!

They move up stage and off at back, as they do so, SILAS *and the* POLECAT
come quickly on, L. 1 E.

SILAS (*much excited*). Say it again—over again! This evening, you
say? It can't be true—it's too good to be true!

POLE. Everything's arranged to take place before the return call.
Their plan is to overpower the guard, and under cover of the moor fog,
that's now rising, scatter and run. (*coughs*) A Dartmoor fog is sudden
but convenient.

SIL. (*aside*). Very convenient! (*aloud*) It's a mad attempt.

POLE. If I hadn't given the office, not so mad as you think. The plans
were laid long ago, and once they'd got the free run of the Moor, they'd
be as hard to find as the fog itself when the sun shines out in the morn-
in'.

SIL. (*placing his hand upon* POLECAT's *shou'der*). Go back to them, and
when the attempt is made, take care that No. 47 is among the mutineers.
Keep close to him—close as wax, and when the moment comes to act,
give me a signal that I may know my man.

POLE. What signal?

SIL. Cough, and cough loudly. Now go, and don't lose sight of him
for a moment. (POLECAT *exits,* L. SILAS *looking after him*) I'll provide
for you, too, my friend. You know too much for Silas Jarrett. (*unslings
the carbine and tries the double barrels with ramrod, laughs*) The cat had
need of nine lives, who pulls my chestnuts from the fire!

While he is speaking, MARGARET *appears behind, looks anxiously round, then
comes down.*

MARGARET. Sir! (SILAS *turning, starts, and recoils.* MARGARET *greatly
agitated*) You are an officer of the prison, (*pressing purse into his hand*)
take this—don't count i—there is more, much more, I am sure, than
you would ask; but answer me a question.

SIL. (*who has lowered peak of cap, and in a rough voice*). What question?

Mar. You know Robert Arnold, a prisoner ?

Sil. No. 47. Yes.

Mar. Can I speak to him—but for five minutes ?

Sil. (*motioning, as he would give back purse*). No ; against regulations.

Mar. You shall speak for me then, you are an honest man, and it is from honest lips I would have Robert Arnold hear the good news. To-morrow he will be free—we're only waiting for the necessary papers from London, but I would spare him another night of agony. (*grasping him by sleeve*) Pray, don't refuse me this favor—but whisper it in his ear—say that the lives he has preserved, are devoted to his service. His innocence is known—that there is one who can identify the real criminal—tell him that justice is already on his track, and—but why do you turn away ? Say this for me, I implore you—and I will double your reward to-morrow—I am rich.

Sil. (*with momentary forgetfulness*). Rich ! You ! (*correcting himself*) 'Tis rare, indeed, to find rich ladies taking an interest in one of our black sheep.

Mar. Ah ! but I tell you Robert Arnold is one whose innocence can be proved. However, you shall run no danger for me, I will go to the governor.

Sil. (*stopping her*). No, no, there's no necessity. I'll do what you ask—trust in me—and—and—No. 47, shall know the good fortune that's in store for him.

Mar. I shall not forget your kindness. What is your name !

Sil. Oh, for so slight a service, I'm amply rewarded already. The real culprit is known, you say.

Mar. By a strange chance he was discovered on board ship by the very person he had robbed !

Sil. Who arrested him, of course ?

Mar. No, he escaped by leaping overboard.

Sil. He was drowned, then ?

Mar. We have learnt that he was picked up and landed at a small port on the Devon coast—but I must rejoin my friends. (*moves a little up stage—again pauses, and turns towards* Silas, *taking locket from neck*) Stay—give Robert this locket ; it contains the hair of the mother and the child whose lives he preserved, and who have ever remembered his name in their prayers. [*She exits, c. platform, and off* R., *at back.*]

Sil. (*makes a prolonged whistle of dismay*). My luck again ! Fore-warned, forearmed though. (*opens locket while speaking, and reads*) " Margaret and Alice." Two locks of hair intertwined—one dark as night— that's Margaret's ; the other, like a ray of sunlight—that's the little Alice's, I suppose. (*short laugh*) Curse the sentiment ! I wish the case was heavier. However, I'm not too proud to refuse the unexpected donation, so in it goes to my jewel-box ; and now to put my brother warders on the alert.

As he goes off, Convicts *re-appear in various parts, under guardianship of* Warders, *as before.* Warders *pace stage at back, appearing and disappearing.* Snipe, *who has contrived to place himself so as to work close to* Arnold—*as before, down stage—speaks in a low quick voice.*

Jack. Keep your eyes and ears open, 47 ; it's Isaac Vidler as gives the word. They'd have given it long ago, but they were afraid o' you.

As he speaks Convicts *begin to group stealthily in c. of stage, some as sentinels watching* Warders *off stage ; each time the* Warders *re-appear, the men scatter and make a feint of being hard at work*

Rob. Of me ?

Jack. New comers are always suspicious, and as you seemed to hold your head so high they thought no good of you, but *I* squared it by swearing as you were a regular out-and-outer—one of them desprit coves as 'ud scrag their own grandmother for her silver thimble. Oh, no thanks; when I takes to a cove he's sure of my good word.

Rob. *(aside).* Escape from here ? yes, at *all* hazards. No friend who ever knew me in the past shall see me in this dress again. *(murmur increases among* Convicts *at back—they draw close together and come down stage.)*

Jack *(much excited).* Here comes old Vidler—a patri-arch, as has grown gray in prisons; but shut him up as they will, Isaac is like the measle. —he's always breakin' out.

Crowd of Convicts *separate to give passage to* Isaac Vidler, *an old, wrinkled convict in " bad conduct " dress and fetter on leg. His head, when he moves his cap, is bald, but his grizzled brows hang over his sharp gleaming eyes. His figure is slightly bent, and he has a way of rubbing his hands together, with a low, chuckling laugh. The* Polecat *stands near him, coughing at intervals behind his hand—his manner cringing, but eagerly watchful.*

Isaac *(putting back crowd with extended hands as he advances).* Let me breathe, my children, let me breathe. You're a bad lot—a very bad lot, but you wouldn't rob the old man of his breath, would yer ?

Convicts. No, no ! *(the* Polecat *coughs as he catches sight of* Silas, *visible for a moment among the rocks.)*

Isaac *(turning sharply).* Stop that cough, Polecat ! or I'll find you a lozenger that shall b: " cough-no-more " with a vengeance ! *(to* Convicts) Then it's agreed, my flowers o' beauty, that we wants a change o' air ?

Jack. We can't do without it.

Pole. Prisons, isn't what they used to be !

Jack *(oratorically).* They're a-cuttin' us down with the rest of the Government establishments. If things ain't made more comfortable, how can they expect us to s:op ? *(plaintively)* Once the old instituoshun's gone, and—*(throwing wide arms)* where are we ? *(murmur of approbation, which he suppresses—*Polecat *coughs again under cover of the excitement, and* Silas *again appears and disappears among rocks, after exchanging signal)* Patri-arch ! if I may be permitted to advise——

Isaac *(snappishly).* No, yer mayn't. *(addressing* Convicts) I takes the lead or I washes my hands of th: business. Is there anyone here as can say he knows more of a prison th:n Isaac V:dler ? *(amidst an ab shed silence* Isaac *draws himself up with great dignity)* It's not for me to boast of my f m'ly, but si ce George the Third was king, there hasn't been a Vid:er, ma:e or fem:le, as hasn't enjoyed the hospitality of the British Government ! So shut up, my hemp blossoms ! and if the old man's to pilot the sh ip, he does it his own way.

All. Hear, hear !

Isaac. Unfort'nately, my bless:ed bab:es in the wood ! you are here, and it's just where you don't want to be *(turning with a fierce gesture to* Polecat) Stop that cough ! d:ye h:ar ? *(the deep booming of prison bell heard)* There goes the return bel:! *(to the* Convicts *watching at back)* The warders will be here in a moment, k:ep your eyes skinned and your hands ready, my dandelions ! and now, as I'm tired of public speaking, do you, Jack, tell 'em the way they must take, if they wishes to return to the buzzums of their affectionate families.

JACK (*the* CONVICTS *group round him as he speaks, with outstretched necks, devouring his words*). All right, Patri-arch. Fust, then, you catches hold of one of them branches--(*pointing to tree on rising ground or hill to* R.) a-top of that heap of bou'ders, and make a drop into the gully below. (*some of the* CONVICTS *draw back and give a whistle of alarm*) When. if you haven't broken your necks, as I did pretty near, when I tumbled into it t'other day—you'll keep along down 'mong the fuzz-s and bushes till you comes to a deep hole—where you'l get another cropper if you don't take care—at tho bottom you c eeps and crawls till you finds yourself in the deserted workings of an old lead mine, and then I leaves you to take your chance of coming out somehow or somewheres, and take advantage of the night fog to make tracks for the coast.

FIRST CONVICT (*shaking head*). It's a tick.ish job—who leads the way?

SECOND CONVICT (*drawing back*). There's a fall of thirty feet to begin with!

OTHER CONVICTS (*also drawing back*). Yes, who goes fust?

VID. (*with an air of superb generosity*). As Jack Snipe discovered the road, he shall have the first chance!

JACK. Of breaking his neck! thank'ye, Patri-arch. (*grandly*) I accept with one proviso! (*laying hand on* ARNOLD'S *shoulder*) that No.-47 is the pal as goes with me. (*quick—aside to* ARNOLD) Trust me, I know the way and the workings, and I m sure as a cat it's liberty any way!

As JACK *and* ARNOLD *cross quickly.* POLECAT *coughs violently, and* SILAS *is seen to appear and disappear on boulders at left. Then the* CONVICTS, *who have been watching in different attitudes behind, come quickly down stage.*

CONVICTS. The screws! the warders! the warders!

VID. (*all activity, and springing on rock*. There's only half a dozen on 'em! At 'em, my tiger lilies! give it 'em hot—and then for a rush!

The CONVICTS, *armed with picks and other mining tools, attack and keep off* WARDERS, *driving them back. At the same time* JACK *and* ARNOLD *have reached top of hill on right, closely followed by the* POLECAT, *who crawls after them rapidly—keeping low down among rocks, like a snake.* JACK *swings himself by branch, and drops immediately,* ARNOLD *catches branch as it rebounds, and is following his example, when* POLECAT, *suddenly springing up from the low brushwood, which has hidden his advance, endeavors to detain him,* ARNOLD *eludes his grasp and disappears amidst the sound of breaking branches and a shower of leaves. The* POLECAT, *who springs into his place is shot from off stage,* L.

SILAS (*entering* L.. *musket in hand*) No. 47! It's No. 47! he was escaping! (*dropping but of musket on ground*) and he's dead!

MARGARET (*who, with* ST. CLAIR *has entered at back,* C., *rushes forward*). No. 47! dead! (*she rushes up the rocks and bends over body*) Dead! No! (*rising up with a joyful cry*) Robert Arnold has escaped!

While MARGARET *is rushing up rocks,* SILAS JARRETT, *whose cap has fallen off, comes quickly down stage and faces* ST. CLAIR, *who, in following* MARGARET, *has taken* C. *The recognition is mutual, and as* ST. CLAIR *raises his finger to denounce him,* SILAS, *down stage* L., *recoils thunderstruck, dropping musket.*

TABLEAU.—*The back ground filled by* WARDERS *who present muskets. The* CONVICTS *clustering down stage,* R., *and casting aside weapons in token of submission, as Act closes. Curtain descends rapidly. It rises again almost as rapidly and shows change of tableau.* ST. CLAIR *upon hill, half supporting* MARGARET, *and pointing to* SILAS, *who, is in custody, is between two armed* WARDERS, *while* TRUMBLE, C., *is in conversation with* GOVERNOR, *as explaining situation. The* CONVICTS *are sullenly forming into file, under the menacing attitude of* WARDERS.

CURTAIN.

ACT III.

INDIA—A.D., 1857.

SCENE.—*Bhurtpoor, a military post and trading out-station on the banks of the Jumna.*

As curtain draws up SERGEANT WATTLES *comes down with* TRIGGS *and* POLLY, *the two latter shaking him heartily by the hand.*

TRIGGS. I'm so glad to see yer!

POLLY. When did you come?

WATTLES. About an hour ago; and a hot march we've had of it, the country's swarming with rebels—and for the devils who have cut off our little detachment, and driven us in here, we'll give a good account of 'em, never fear.

POL. Fear! Joe Triggs is brave as a lion; I've heard him say so, often.

TRIG. Yes, certainly, but that was when I was a fraction of the British army, now having bought myself out and taken a clerkship with Mr. Arnold, that I might be near you, Polly, I've dropped the lion, and (*endeavoring to take her waist*) cottoned to the lamb.

POL. Have done, sir! how dare you, and the sergeant present!

TRIG. Don't, Polly, don't turn your back to me in that broad way! Who could resist such a wide expanse of English waist land?

WAT. Don't make a stranger of me. There's nothing I admire so much as love-making, or a marriage, always provided I'm only a spectator. But I want you to tell me all about Robert Arnold; I heard something of the story when our regiment was back in England—it was quite a romance.

TRIG. Ro-mance!

POL. You never read nothing so interesting even in the "London Journal."

TRIG. After making his escape from Dartmoor, quite ignorant of the steps that were being taken for his release, he got away on ship-board and worked his passage out to India, here, after no ends of ups and downs, he hears of his innocence having been proved, and of the arrest of that skulking, ne'er-do-well, Silas Jarrett!

WAT. Silas Jarrett! who's Silas Jarrett?

TRIG. Lor! *you* ought to remember him! The drunken chap as you wanted to 'list, when Polly's cruelty driv' me to take the shilling ten year ago in Southampton.

WAT. Ten years ago! (*touching forehead*) Don't answer to call—wiped off the muster-roll of memory.

POL. Him as was the living, breathing image——

TRIG. (*interrupting*). Less the rags and dirt.

POL. Of your captain, Mr. Ormond Willoughby.

WAT. (*with dignity*) Colonel, Sir Ormond Willoughby—got the title on the death of his brother; he's as rich as Crœsus, whoever that chap may be, but what's become of Silas, him as did the robbery for which Robert—I mean Mr. Arnold, was condemned?

TRIG. He was trounced for that and some other little affairs of the same character, and is now working out his fifteen year in Australy. But I say, Wattles——

WAT. Sergeant Wattles! keep up the respect though you have left the army.

TRIG. Confidence for confidence—without prejudice, you know, as we used to say in the law—what's all this about Sir Ormond and Miss Alice Armitage?

WAT. That the colonel proposed marriage at Madras and was accepted, only the match were put off as Miss Alice was too young.

POL. (*surprised*). Accepted! not by Miss Alice?

WAT. Same thing—he was accepted by her guardian, Mr. St. Clair.

TRIG. Our resident collector—that is to say, who *was* our resident collector, for he's now again away at Madras on business.

POL. Leaving Miss Alice under the care of my mistress, Mrs. Doctor Honoria McTavish. Have done, Joe, will you? I hear Mr. Jack's voice in the counting-house.

WAT. Who's Mr. Jack?

POL. Oh! such a duck of a man!

TRIG. Duck of a man! there you go again, Miss Dobbs, it's your nature to be expansive, even in your compliments. After all, who is Mr. Jack? what is Mr. Jack? Mr. Jack is only Mr. Arnold's factotum! Mr. Arnold's confidential servant, who takes a position no one knows why, and comes from no one knows where—that's what Mr. Jack is. (*bugle calls heard at* L. *side.*)

ALL. What's that for?

WAT. Nothing. nothing. (*aside, as he crosses stage*). Mustn't alarm them, but something's up.

TRIG. You ain't going, sergeant?

WAT. (*at side as bugles sound again*) Duty before pleasure, my children. (*aside, as he exits* C. *and* L.) The scouts have come in—we shall have hot work before long.

POL. (*going*). And I must be off, too.

TRIG. (*bitterly*). To talk to Mr. Jack. Cruelty, thy name is Dobbs; but what can I expect, when even the sun of India has failed to melt you.

POL. You'll break my heart, Joe.

TRIG. I wish I could, but I'm not a stonemason.

POL. I won't hear any one speak against Mr. Jack; and, though he certainly never speaks of his life in England, yet he's everything a man should be.

TRIG. Is he? an undersized, brown-visaged feller!

POL. Who has always a kind for——

JACK *entering from counting-house,* L., *has come quietly down, his appearance is much changed from previous act, he is no longer the cadaverous convict with the close-cropped hair, he wears whiskers and his face is browned, he has the usual light colonial costume, slightly exaggerated.*

JACK. One of his own countrywomen, and really, Miss Dobbs, to see such a face and figure as yours in this land of rice and curry powder, is to think of strawberries and cream, fresh butter and new laid eggs, streaky bacon, ginger beer, and all other kind of dairy produce.

Pol. You don't like India, Mr. Jack?

Jack. (R.). Like it! Do you take me for a tiger, or what's worse, for one o' these gamboge colored ragamuffins, who are rampaging about the country, a warring with babies and women. 'Ere's a costume for a man as has known what cord'roy and fust'in means, and has enjoyed a real London fog (aside and winking) and a Dartmoor one too! Lor! I get quite cold when I think of it—even in this bakehouse of a place!

Pol. (c). But the Indian sunshine!

Jack. Bother the Injun sunshine! Hasn't our English women got a better article in their eyes—though if all heyes was like yourn, Miss Dobbs, they'd singe us into hashes!

Trig. (who has been fuming about, interposes between them). Beg pardon! but you are not as yet appointed overlooker to this estate, Mr. Jack.

Jack. If I've offended the lady I apologize, but when in the Inj es we do as the Injuns do, and a little hextra warmth is allowable.

Pol. (bridling). Offend me, not a bit of it; I know how to take care of myself under all conditions of the atmosphere, but when I do want a special constable I shan't send for you. Joe Triggs. (she goes up stage.)

Jack (to Triggs). There, there, you've been and gone and done it, Joe Triggs, if you will do the tyrant and hinterfere with the little fancies of the sex, Joe Triggs, why don't you stop till you're married, Joe Triggs?

Trig. Married! thank you, I don't see it; if Miss Dobbs must bring down game she shan't do it with a certificate.

Pol. (coming down like a hurricane). What do you mean by that, sir? (hysterically) You, you want to insult me! (staggering back and sinking suddenly against Jack) I throw myself on your protection, Mr. Jack! (aside) I'll give Joe a lesson!

Jack (aside). I wish she wouldn't throw herself so heavily.

Trig. Protection indeed! It is I who should apply for that. (touching breast) It's all bankruptcy here, Miss Dobbs—all bankruptcy, I assu e you.

Pol. Then why don't you take your declaration off the file and give better people a chance?

Jack (exultingly). Better people, Joe Triggs, better people.

Trig. Better! (aside) I can't stand that. (to Jack, who is looking off) Mr. Jack!

Jack (turning round). Sir, to you.

Trig. (eyeing him over with intense grandeur). We shall meet again!

Jack (offering hand). De-lighte l!

Trig. (trying to get at Jack, who avoids him behind Polly) Where the intervention of a third party will be impossible.

Pol. (aside and delighted) He's working himself up like new beer. (stopping Triggs as he is going up stage) What is the matter, Joe?

Trig. (suddenly breaking down). Oh, nothing to speak of; it's the buzzum, miss, the buzzum, that's all. The Triggs's was always tender—tender, though brought up to the law! This is the spot where our fam'ly feels, Miss Dobbs, in the buzzum, this side o' the weskit—here! (he strikes breast violently, and rushes off c. to L.)

Jack. Oh, Miss Dobbs, if it hadn't been for you I should have killed him. Did you see how he ran, when I went like this? (puces himself in a ridiculous attitude—approaching Polly, who stands aghast) What's the matter with him, Polly?

Pol. (turning upon him). Matter, sir—matter! I'd have you to know

that true love is not a matter to be sniggered at and made fun of.
You've made us both unhappy, that's what you've done. (*begins to sob.*)

JACK. Done! what have I done?

POL. Haven't you made love to me before Joe? (*sobs again*) But you
men are always so stupid!

JACK. I say, don't! you'll become too moist if you go on in that way
—if I did make love to you, I give you my word of honor, I didn't mean
it—I swear I didn't mean it!

POL. (*stopping crying suddenly*). You didn't! you didn't! (*giving him a
sounding box of the ears*) Then that will teach you not to come between
two loving hearts again! (*as she exits* R.) Men have no feelin's!

JACK (*rubbing his ear*). No feelin's! That woman doesn't know her
own power.

As he speaks, the laughing face of ALICE ARMITAGE *appears at the half opened
trelliced window above verandah, amongst the creeping plants and roses.*

And now to see Mr. Arnold, who's gone down to the stores to arm as
many of our coffee-colored friends as may prove faithful in case of attack. (*seriously*) And by what I seed this morning you may count them
on your finger tips. (ALICE, *who has plucked a handful of flowers, from the
plant about window, throws them at* JACK *without their touching or being
perceived by him*) Ah! Robert Arnold! when I think of what he's done
for me and the risk he still runs 'acos for me—I'd—I'd—— (*as he raises
his hand to give emphasis, a little satin slipper, which* ALICE *has taken off,
hits him in the back—with a jump he straightens himself up*) Wot's that?
(*picks up slipper*) Ah! you come from Miss Alice, there isn't such
another tiny little trotter this side of the Thames, though Heaven forgive me speaking of that blessed river, with its Isle of Dogs, and ile-y
fogs, alongside of his cursed place, all blue and yeller like a bad cheese,
or a poached heg.

ALICE (*whispering over balcony*). Hist! Mr. Jack.

JACK (*in centre, bending over slipper, back towards her, speaks aside*). I
hears yer! It's one o' them voices that even to hear is a priwilege.

ALICE. Mr. Jack.

JACK (*still without turning*). She's up to some m'schief, some bit of
wickedness, and she'll get me into it as sure as eggs is eggs! She's
generalissimo, and when she says, "Jack, *do it!*" Jack does it, mind
yer! (*turning*) Yes, there she is, one o' them bits o' heaven as we can't
'elp b essin' whensoever and howsomder we sees 'em.

ALICE (*stamping foot*). Why don't you answer?

JACK (*eagerly*). Don't throw t'other slipper, Miss, you'll catch cold.
(*aside*) She's capable of chucking her whole wardrobe. (*aloud*) What do
ye vant, miss?

ALICE (*pettishly*). I want to get out—I'm locked up.

JACK. Who locked you up?

ALICE. Mrs. McTavish——

JACK (*aside*). She's a dragon, she is.

ALICE. She says, there's going to be a battle—a *dreadful* battle.

JACK (*with sudden seriousness*). Well, miss——

ALICE (*clapping hands*). An I I want to see it——

JACK (*turning round, in half aside*). *She* wants to see it. She talks of
a battle as if it were a bit of barley sugar. (*aloud*) Where's the key,
miss?

ALICE. In Mrs. McTavish's pocket.

JACK. Then I collapses and shuts up like a two foot rule——

ALICE. You won't help me?

JACK. I would if I could—but——

ALICE. You won't help me—you wont?

JACK (*emphatically*). I can't.

ALICE. Then I'll help myself—and down I come—— (*as she speaks, she prepares to descend by creeping plants around pillars of verandah.*)

JACK (*greatly excited and rushing to her as she descends*). Oh, I say don't! What are you up to—that is, I mean, what are you coming down to? You'll hurt your precious little tootsy, it's without a slipper. Oh, lor'! oh, lor'! here, lean on me; gently does it! But what a hass I am! (*placing her carefully on ground*) As if you could do a thing as wasn't the gentlest of the gentles!

ALICE (*hopping about*). Jack, give me my slipper.

JACK (*as he put. it on, she resting her foot upon his knee*). Ah! what wouldn't Mr. Arnold give to be in my place?

ALICE (*pulling away her foot*). If you talk like that—I'll—I'll—tell Mrs. McTavish that you let me out! (*with sudden change of manner—in great alarm, looking off,* R. U. E.) Here she comes—hide me!

JACK. Oh, but miss, where am I to hide you? Here, get behind a flower.

ALICE (*stamping her foot imperatively*). Hide me, I tell you! (*running behind verandah*) And get rid of Mrs. McTavish.

JACK (*aside, as he places her behind a creeping plant in corner of verandah*). It's weak, I know, but the chap as says " no " to her is a beast.

He is moving up stage as MRS. McTAVISH *and* ARNOLD *appear at back,* R. U. E.

ALICE (*thrusting her head through leaves*). Do take her away, Mr. Jack.

JACK (*aghast*). Take her away? *Me!* take her away? Oh, lor'! how am I to do it?

ALICE (*coaxingly*). Oh, do! there's a good, dear Jack! Talk to her in Scotch, you know. I want to speak to Mr. Arnold, par-tic-u-leer-a-leeraly!

JACK. I understand! But I can't talk Scotch.

He moves up stage as MRS. McTAVISH *and* ROBERT ARNOLD *come down.* ROBERT *wears beard and moustache, carries a rifle in his hand, the strap of which he fastens about shoulder while he speaks.*

ROBERT. I fear the worst, Mrs. McTavish; and would give all of which I am possessed if every woman in Bhurtpoor were now in Calcutta.

MRS. McT. An' d'ye think these loons will have the owdacity to attack the station?

ROB. Sir Ormond Willoughby, who has just arrived, and takes command of the cantonment, thinks it more than likely, they are in the neighborhood, and in large force.

MRS. McT. The deevils!

ROB. (*anxiously*). Where is Miss Armitage?

MRS. McT. (L. C.). In her ain room, (*aside, touching pocket*) under lock and key. (*as she speaks,* ALICE'S *laughing face is protruded from among the flowers, and after a quick gesture to both* ARNOLD *and* JACK, *is again withdrawn.*)

JACK (R. C., *coming down stage, touches* MRS. McTAVISH *on arm and speaks in a whisper*). Ay, Mistress McTavish, there's a' the soger's wives ben the house asking for ye.

MRS. McT. (*sharply*). What for?

JACK. Ay, I canna say for certain ! but they say the medicine chest has a' gane wrong, and they doot the perscriptions.

MRS. McT. Doot the preescreeptions ! An' every one o' them wreetin' out in the learned languages by the late Dr. McTavish, M.D., F.R. S.S. !

JACK (*aside*). And S T U P I D ! Better go right through the alphabet while you're about it. (*aloud*) It's like their impudence—and I tel, 'em so. That Mrs. Flanagan says that you canna read your ain labels, and that you've given her an embrocation to swallow in twa doses.

MRS. McT. Where is she ?

JACK. Ay, she's been to the house, and Mrs. Flanagan says your— your—— (*he cannot think of any more Scotch, so rattles out*) " So Willie brew'd a peck o' maut," " What's a' the steer, kimmer," Rob Roy and Tullockgorum.

MRS. McT. The ungrateful hussy ! Didn't I attend her husband in his last moments ?

JACK (*highly delighted at the success of ruse*). This way, mum, this way ! I think I see her over there by the barrack door ! Ay, they are all swallowing the sticking-plaster. (*exit* MRS. McTAVISH, R. 2 E. JACK, *with a glance of triumph at* ALICE) Well, I've got rid of Mistress McTavish for you.

ALICE (*coming down*). Oh, I'm so glad to have the opportunity of speaking to you alone ; but if you look so glum as that, I won't say a word !

ROB. (*coming down*, R. C.). Dear Alice, if you only knew the weight on my heart—I don't know what to do !

ALICE (L. C.). But I do ! I'm going to speak to Sir Ormond Willoughby myself.

ROB. You !

ALICE. Haven't you said he is the noblest of men ?

ROB. I've every reason to believe it.

ALICE. Then be sure he'll act up to his reputation. Half the mischief in this world is made by people not having things put before them in their proper light. When poor, dear mamma made Mr. St. Clair my guardian, I promised to obey him, of course ; but then, equally, of course, I never expected he'd ask me to do anything I didn't like.

ROB. This dreadful rebellion has been a heavy blow to Mr. St. Clair, and it is said that but for Sir Ormond's assistance he'd be now a ruined man. Sir Ormond Willoughby now offers you a princely home in England, while I—— (*taking both her hands*) You know my past, Alice ?

ALICE (*with feeling*). And do you think I could ever have loved you so much if I hadn't known it ? Yours was the name that my dear mother taught me utter in my prayers ; and, being always in my mouth, i:— it—it—somehow got down into my heart, and there's an end of it.

ROB (*still holding her hands and raising them to his lips*). You color everything with your own bright nature, Alice ; but as I have said, St. Clair is under deep obligations to Sir Ormond Willoughby.

ALICE. And how does that affect me ?

ROB. (*dropping her hands and half turning away*). And greater, a thousand times greater are the obligations I'm under to Mr. St. Clair.

ALICE (*slowly*). I see ; the refusal must come from him—I will manage that.

As she speaks COLONEL SIR ORMOND WILLOUGHBY *enters,* R. U. E., *in undress, and* CIVILIANS, *with* SERGEANT WATTLES, *all armed, enter hastily at back,* C.

COLONEL (*speaking to* ARNOLD, *who advances up stage,* ALICE *remaining down stage near verandah*). How many of your people can you rely on, Arnold?

ROB. Few, I fear.

JACK (*entering,* R. 2 E.). None. The copper-colored scum have struck work to a man.

ROB. This must be seen to. (*going up stage with* JACK.)

COL. (*to* WATTLES). Sergeant, accompany Mr. Arnold. (*to* CIVILIANS) Gentlemen, this is a matter that concerns us all—your wives and families. Give Mr. Arnold your aid I entreat you. (*they all pass out—aside, as he comes down stage*) I dare not hint the extent of the danger. If the fugitive bands have united, we shall be scattered like a handful of sand. They blockade every road, yet, if I could but convey the news of our peril to the general's camp, we might still hope for relief. It will be a mission of life and death—almost certain death, and therefore to be undertaken by myself. (*as he turns to move up stage, he comes face to face with* ALICE—*removing cap*) Miss Armitage! Alice.

ALICE. Oh, Colonel Willoughby, can I have a few minutes' conversation with you?

COL. I fear not now, but when the danger that threatens us is over—not that there is any real danger to alarm you—but——

ALICE (*seriously*). I know the full extent of the danger that threatens —and it is at *such* a time, when young and old alike tremble between life and death—that I would speak of a matter that *is* life and death to me.

COL. (*astonished?*). Alice!

ALICE. My guardian, Mr. St. Clair, has been more than a benefactor to my family—he has been it's saviour. He is also under great obligations to you! You are rich and I am comparatively poor—with Mr. St. Clair's approval you have honored me with the offer of your hand.

COL. (*fervently*). An offer, Alice, which I trust——

ALICE. Oh! if you speak in that way I shall break down before I've got half through what I have to say.

COL. (*laughing*). And what's that? I'm a soldier, Alice, and can stand fire!

ALICE. It's only that I want you to give up all idea of marrying me— and also I want you to take upon yourself all responsibility of breaking off the match.

COL. (*much startled*). Miss Armitage!

ALICE (*naively*). Of course, I know it can't be any *great* sacrifice to you, because we're almost strangers to each other!

COL. (*much pained*). Excuse me, Miss Armitage, but I have passed the age of light fancies and fickle determinations.

ALICE. Oh! I'm sure I feel greatly flattered and honored—and I dare say I might have been proud and happy if—— (*she hesitates.*)

COL. Well! "if"——

ALICE. If I hadn't loved somebody else!

COL. Does Mr. St. Clair know of this?

ALICE. Nobody knows anything about it, but myself and Robert!

COL. (*starting back*). Robert Arnold! Impossible!

ALICE (*with dignity*). The choice I have made, Sir Ormond Willoughby, carries with it no disgrace to me and no insult to you! I was early taught that I owe I my life, and what was more to me, my mother's life, to Robert Arnold. (*she breaks out again in her natural gay, sunny way*) And so, somehow, you see, I grew to love him even before I knew what the word love really meant. Young as I am I know the honor reflected by a great name, a name such as yours, Sir Ormond; yet were Robert

Arno'd as obscure and penniless as he was when his name was first breathed into my childish ears, I would choose him above all others that the world contains—I dare say you think me romantic, imprudent, silly, if you will, but—(*drawing herself up*) I love Robert Arnold! I love him with all my heart! (*as* WILLOUGHBY *turns away with a despairing gesture, and as to hide his emotion,* ALICE, *advancing, lays her hand quickly on his arm*) You mustn't think me heartless or unfeeling, but Robert is so unhappy, and I—I—(*brushing tears from eyes*) am so very, very miserable, and we can never be happy unless you help us. I know it's my guardian's ambition I should be your wife, and—and—he's under great obligations to you, so that——

COL. (*with generous warmth, and taking both her hands*). Oh! you mustn't speak of that—I'll be your friend, Alice, though—(*with an effort*) I'd have given him half my fortune had it been otherwise——

ALICE. You'll be my friend then?

COL. It's a heavy sacrifice, but a true love should shrink from no sacr'fice. (*raising her hands to his lips*) And both Robert and yourself shall find a true friend in me.

Rattle of drums off scene—WILLOUGHBY *dropping her hands and moving a step or two up stage as* ROBERT ARNOLD, WATTLES, OFFICERS, *and* CIVILIANS *enter, hurriedly, c. from* R. *and* L.

What's the meaning of this?

ROBERT. The rebels have crossed the river in force! (*sound as of distant discharge of artillery*) and have begun the attack.

COL. (*rapidly aside to* ARNOLD, *and grasping his hand, comes down stage*). Robert! to your care I entrust Miss Armitage. (*taking stage as he goes up, and addressing the armed men who group behind*) Gentlemen! if we are but few in numbers, let us be strong in our heart! Balk the tiger in his first spring, and you may beat him back into the jungle with your knotted handkerchiefs.

Up stage, SIR ORMOND *turns with an assuring gesture to* ALICE, *who is now clinging to* ROBERT's *arm, and, amidst an enthusiastic cheer and clash of arms, the tableau is closed in by*

SCENE II.—*Interior of* MR. ST. CLAIR's *Bungalow—the sun blind of verandah down, c. At intervals, sounds of firing, as at a great distance.*

POLLY *rushes on,* L., *her hands to ears, in great alarm, followed by* TRIGGS, *endeavoring to console her.*

TRIGGS. Polly—but I say, Polly, listen to reason.

POLLY. I shan't!

TRIG. Of course you won't, and I was wrong to expect it of yer. Cast your cruel eyes on this. (*showing gun which he carries.* POLLY *half turns round, gives a scream, and again averts her face*) Oh, I say! come, draw it mild; you won't win the race by such a false start as that. You've been through your military exercise long ago. (*bitterly*) Ah! I know the sort of arms you like, only you'd have 'em round your waist instead of in your hands.

POL. (*turning upon him like a tigress, her arms a-kimbo*). What do you mean by that, sir? Say that again and I'll box your ears!

TRIG. Oh, Polly! can you speak to me like this, when I shall soon be face to face with gunpowder?

POL. (*softening*). Then why do you go? Can't we both hide in the cellar?

TRIG. The temptation's great, I confess, but I'm an Englishman!

POL. Then try to remain one.

TRIG. My country calls me.

POL. Then let her keep on calling.

TRIG. But some one must answer the *knocks*, Polly.

POL. Well, as far as these chaps are concerned, I wish they was run-a-way ones.

POLLY *crosses to* R   *Noise as of a smash off stage.* POLLY *springs away from* TRIGGS, *they having approached each other.* JACK SNIPE, *who is armed at all points, enters, hastily,* R.

JACK (*clinging hold of* JOE'S *arm and half fainting with fear*). Don't be alarmed, don't be alarmed! It's only a shell that's entered the kitchen and knocked over a coffee service—that's all! which reminds me, Polly, that Mrs. McTavish has just fainted, and is now shouting for you.

POL. (*with sudden alarm*). I'll go to her.

JACK. Oh, never mind her—she can take care of herself—but just go and see after Miss Alice, who's crying her little 'art out on the sofa.

POL. (*as she runs off,* R.). Bless her! if *she* take on she'll cry my heart out too. (*shots. They both seek support in each other's backs.*)

JACK. Don't be alarmed, Joe, I'm with you—I'll never leave you.

TRIG. (*asking round confidentially*). How do you feel, Mr. Jack?

JACK. Well, as—as—speaking man to man yer know—not so well as I expected. These chaps don't fire far enough off. I'm not a coward, not naturally, as far as a black eye goes, but—but perhaps it's constitoo-shun il; I like to fight with plenty on my side.

TRIG. (*taking his hand*). I respect your feelin's!

JACK (*returning the grasp with ferror*). And shares 'em, I know—we're not made of common clay, Mr. Triggs—not pipe clay, you know. Delicate minds shrink from observation, and I don't mind confessing to you, that if left to myself I would have the moral courage to choose the rear.

TRIG. We must have been born under the same planet! I'll stick to you like a mussel to a rock. (*as he is about to embrace* JACK, *he suddenly stops*) But how about Miss Dobbs?

JACK. What of her?

TRIG. You like her?

JACK. Of course I do.

TRIG. You love her?

JACK. Get out! Love! Look you here! A man loves as he *must*, not as he chooses. For *my* part, there's been only three human creeturs as have ever warmed me up to that point. The fust, was a little chip of a child—as, happily for itself p'raps—died afore it could know how dear it was to me. The second as was Mr. Arnold, as has stuck and will stick here, (*touching heart*) mind yer—as bright and as fast as a pin in a pin cushion—and last of the three is Miss Alice, who's a-cryin' herself blind for one as I knows on—even to see them together in poetry—

       " If you loves me as I loves you,

       No knife shall cut our loves in two."—" *Shakespear.*"

TRIG. (*delighted*). Then you don't love Polly?

JACK. Make your mind easy! It was only *my* fun! a chap must amuse himself somehow! But once you places her afore me as Mrs. Triggs, I wouldn't touch her with a pair of tongs! 'Pon my soul I wouldn't!

TRIG. (*indignantly*). What do you mean?

JACK (*very kindly, and as wishing to kill an ill-feeling*). She's not my sort! Too much of her——

TRIG. (*with difficulty restraining his passion*). Indeed!

JACK (*same amiable business*). Besides—if I did love her, I wouldn't marry her.

TRIG. (*exploding with passion*). What do you mean?

JACK. Oh! bless you! I don't mean what you mean! What I mean is this! that there are circumstances connected with my family history, which I'm not called on to explain; I wouldn't marry any mortal woman.

Enter WATTLES, L., *hastily, in great disorder, musket in hand, followed by* SERVANTS.

WATTLES. What are you loitering here for—are you going to be killed like sheep? The rebels have crossed the river.

TRIG. (*faintly, getting* R. *of* JACK). Crossed it? Oh, lor'!

WAT. It's fearful odds—a hundred to one!

JACK (*dubiously*). One to one is quite odds enough for me.

WAT. You coward! (*going*) Why don't you take example of Arnold! I left him fighting *like* a man, surrounded by scores of sepoys and in deadly peril.

JACK (*springing forward*). What—what's that you say? Robert—Mr. Arnold! oh, curse the mister! Robert Arnold in danger—in deadly peril? (*rushing at the astonished* TRIGGS, *and wresting gun from his hand*) Here, give me hold of that thing of yours! I'll be among 'em before my name's Jack Snipe

WAT. Jack what?

JACK. *Robinson!* I said Jack Robinson. Where's Mr. Robert Arnold?

WAT. You c.n't reach him! He's keeping the fort at the other side of the river.

JACK. Not reach him! I should l ke to see who'll stop me. (*flinging hat on ground, and, grasping gun firmly*) I'm not one of them as looks at a benefactor as if he were only a cold joint in the cupboard, to be cut at when one wants him; I looks at him as something to live and die for —and now the hour is come, I'm blessed if I don't die for him! (*to* SERVANTS, *who stand at side*) Here, make way! I wouldn't advise anyone to stop me now!

TRIG. (*plucking up courage*). Now only look at him—blessed if I don't have a shy, too.

As he rushes out, L. 1 E., followed by the others, the venetian blinds, c., are lifted cautiously, and SILAS JARRETT, *haggard, ragged, and wounded, crawls into the veranduh.*

SILAS. (*after advancing a few steps, and listening*). It's like my luck! Escaped at the hazard of my life from Australia, that land of kangaroos, to the land of curry powder, and only to find myself, as usual out of the frying-pan into the fire—cursed luck! I'd always an ambition to be an Indian prince of some sort, or a rajah, at least. Ha, ha! so as brown seemed to be the winning color, I staked on *that*, like a fool; for suddenly they take it into their heads that I meant to betray them, the stupid rogues! As if I haven't more to fear from capture than they have! I gave them leg bail, and swam the Jumna, with bullets sputtering round me like hailstones, I reached the bank, and, surprised by a party of soldiers, put a bold fy. upon it, and begin with " this is smart work, my lads," expecting a bayonet stab before the words are out of my mouth ; not a bit of it, each chap draws himself up as stiff as a ramrod, and salutes. (*laughs*) Salutes me ? me! I don't stop to ask 'em why, but hurry on, but not before I hear one of 'em whisper " fancy our colonel in that disguise, he's been to have a squint at the enemy ! " Who they *take* me for, I'm ble sed if I know, and as long as I'm not *re-taken*. (*laughs*) I'm blessed if I care. (*starts, listens and with a frightened movement retreats and crouches back against wall*) I thought I heard a footstep ! (*wipes forehead*) How nervous a fellow gets who holds his life by the skin of his teeth, as I've done for the last three months ! (*suddenly crouches down and listens*) It's a woman's step ! I thought *my* ears couldn't deceive me !

A distant discharge of firearms, and ALICE *enters, hurriedly,* R.—SILAS *huddled back, keenly watchful, and crouching against wall.*

ALICE. What terrible firing ! and it seems to come nearer ! Oh ! Robert! Robert! Heaven preserve your life ! It is the dearest thing on earth to me !

SIL. (*aside and creeping forward*). Robert ! a lover or a husband, I suppose. What fools women are.

ALICE. And yet I must look again ! (*she thrusts back her hair, which has become loosened from the comb as she approaches sun-blind.*)

SIL. (*aside, creeping nearer*). I've seen that face before ! But where ? (*another discharge of fire-arms, much nearer,* ALICE, *whose hand is upon the sun-blind, starts back.*)

ALICE (*with a low cry*). Robert ! Robert Arnold ! I haven't even the strength to die with you. (*she sinks back, fainting, and is caught in* SILAS'S *arms*)

SIL. (*as he supports her*). Robert Arnold ! Robert Arnold ! who is she like ! (*bending over her*) Ha ! I've dropped into a hornet's nest indeed ! (*rolling of drums and confusion of voices*) It's a retreat ! and where there's a retreat, there's plunder (*looking into* ALICE'S *insensible face*) You are pretty enough to be an angel, my darling ! but earthly matters are of more importance to me just now. (*takes her off,* L. 1 E.—*loud rattle of artilery.*)

SILAS *re-entering,* L. 1 E.

SIL. Hilloh ! they're shelling the house ! (*standing close against window and glancing off to* L.) I'm sorry for the girl, poor little thing ! but in such times as these I've only one number on my slate—(*laughs as he stands in balcony of verandah, prep ring to spring*) and that's number one !
[*Exit, through blind,* C.

Then scene rapidly draws away and discovers

SCENE III.—*A deserted battle-field in the neighborhood of Bhurtpoor.*

JACK (R. C.). Hurrah ! I've pot'ed another ! That makes the fifth ! Rob. Why, Jack, you're quite a fire-eater, I never thought you'd so much courage.

JACK. Well, you can't be more astonished at it than I am—they says as every bullet has its billet, and I'm blessed when this precious pop popping began, if I didn't think I was the billet for the whole lot of 'em ; but never mind me, sir, let's talk of things of more consequence. Where's Sir Ormond ?

Rob. When I left him he had determined to make a desperate attempt to reach the general, who can't be more than a few miles from here, and hurry reinforcements.

Jack (*who is reloading gun*). I'm afraid, unless somebody or something arrives pretty soon, we're cut grass.

Rob. Our only hope is to get the women and children into the fort and defend it to the last.

Jack (*slapping gun stock*). Which we'll do! (*looking at* Arnold, *approaching him, and placing hand on his arm with change of manner*) You're thinking of Miss Alce, ain't yer?

Rob. (*half averting face*). Always! I can think of nothing else.

Jack. I know what it is, that is, I did know afore the little 'un died. When one o' these innocent things get's into one's heart, they ain't to be picked out like a thorn, mind yer.

Rob. (*offering hand which* Jack *grasps*). You're a good fellow, Jack!

Jack. And if I am, whose fault is that—I mean, who's the merit?

Rob. (*very kindly*). Should I fall——

Jack (*interrupting*). There'll be two on us gone, and no mistake! You've made me what I am; I should be a precious sight wus than nothing without yer! Ha! would yer?

Throwing himself quickly before Arnold, *as a* Sepoy *glides on at back from* R. U. E., *and is about to level musket, but seeing himself discovered, disappears.*

Another o' the warmints! (*rushing up stage, cocking gun*) Don't go! stop where you are, my friend, and you shall have my immediate personal attention. Come along, Mr. Robert, there isn't more than half-a-dozen on 'em.

As Jack *exits*, R. U. E., Colonel Willoughby *appears on mound*, L. 2 E., *badly wounded, and walking with extreme difficulty,* Arnold, *following* Jack, *pauses on seeing* Colonel, *and rushes to his assistance. Shot is heard,* R., *supposed to be from* Jack's *rifle.*

Rob. Sir Ormond! wounded!

Colonel (*faintly, and leaning on* Arnold). To the death! Could I but have reached the river all might have gone well. (*staggers, and is supported down stage by* Robert Arnold, *who places him upon a portion of rock*, R. 2 E., *then unbuttons uniform, endeavors to staunch wound.*)

Col. I'm dying! I feel I'm dying! The villain who fired at me crouched behind a tree and has escaped.

Jack *entering*, R. U. E.

Jack. No, he hasn't. I reckoned up his account—struck the total and give him his receipt in full. (Arnold *makes gesture to* Jack *to keep back as the* Colonel *again, and with difficulty, speaks.*)

Col. Arnold—Arnold—Alice has spoken to me—I know all—all! (*stopping him by a gesture, as he is about to speak, and grasping his hand, then in a whisper*) For her sake you will undertake the task in which I have failed. Unless the general is here within an hour—these demons— (*raising himself up by an effort, and placing his hand upon the shoulder of* Arnold, *who is kneeling*)—will work their will! 'Tis almost certain death. yet——!

Rob. (*rising to his feet*). I would go—and should I drop on the road——

Jack (*coming down*). The message shall be carried on!

COL. (*staggering with difficulty to his feet, draws paper from bosom, which he extends to* ARNOLD). The route is marked here—a moment's hesitation may cost a hundred lives! women and children, but for us defenceless—Go! and heaven speed you!

ARNOLD *returns grasp of hand, passes over mound and disappears,* JACK *is about to follow when a groan from* COLONEL *causes him to pause. The* COLONEL *by an effort drags himself painfully up to rock, and after supporting himself for a moment with difficulty, falls to the right behind it. His head is thrown back against ground, and half his body, from waist downwards, is still in view of* AUDIENCE, *and one arm to which still hangs the uniform, which* ARNOLD *has previously unbuttoned.* [*To manage the situation which follows, a "super," dressed as* COLONEL WILLOUGHBY, *stands prepared behind rock, and falls instead of him to extreme right. The actor playing the two parts, disappears by means of a trap under the stage, and re-appears almost immediately on opposite side as* SILAS JARRETT.]

JACK (*coming down quickly*). He's fainted. (*stoops as glancing at body behind rock*) He's dead! (*looking up aghast*). War's a terrible thing after all. To see a man one moment full of life and vigor, and the next smeared out like a paid tavern score—(*with a shiver*) it's awful! I'm afeared they'll never make a soldier of me. It's the suddenness of the thing as I objects to. (*again glancing at body*) Poor fellar, poor fellar! (*sound as of firing heard in direction where* ARNOLD *has disappeared. Rushing up, and springing on mound*) They've seen Robert! Yes, there he goes head fu't into the river, (*jerks himself about ridiculously—alarmed at every report of rifle*) with a string of black devils peppering after him! (*tossing gun and catching it*) After all, I like it—it quickens the blood; and if I am toppled over, what does it matter what becomes of such poor scum as me?

He rushes off, L.   SILAS JARRETT *appears at extreme back,* R.   *His head appears at first above block of stone, upon which he painfully climbs, then crouches like a lizard, watching and listening.*

SILAS. Yes, the reinforcements have arrived, but they've come by another route. (*as he descends and comes down stage*) My luck again. From England to Australia, in company with Vidler, and that *vindictive* villain, the Polecat, who owed me a grudge for the bullet I put in his leg—I wish it had been in his heart? A nice life of it I had among them till I slipped the chain, got on board ship, and worked my passage out to India. Yes, yes, it's only here, amongst the dead and dying, the boom of the cannon, and the clash of steel, that I may hope to be passed over and forgotten. It has been a thundering good fight, though—the very stream I paused to quench my thirst at left a red stain on my lips A grand fight—a tussel between bull-dog and wild cat ; (*distant roll of drum*) and, as usual, the bull dog has had the best of it. (*as he moves up stage he starts*) Hilloh, somebody behind the rock ! (*approaching stealthily*) An officer! (*stooping, he gently pulls the uniform coat, which comes off the extended arm*) Phew! gold swabs too! (*leans over as looking attentively at face—starts violently as recognizing it, then with another whistle of surprise*) Ormond Willoughby! the swell captain they used to chaff me about in Southampton! (*as if a sudden thought had struck him—looks at his own hands, passes one of them quickly over his face, looks again at body, then casts a hurried glance over his own figure*) It would be a desperate game to play—it's worth the trial. (*coming a little down stage, the uniform coat in his hand*) What have I to lose? what have I to gain? Momentary safety, perhaps, and opportunity of escape. Now I know why those fellows saluted me, even in these rags. (*searching pockets of uniform as he speaks*) Yes, I'll do it! (*casting aside his own ragged garment—he commences to invest himself in the* COLONEL'S *uniform, speaking rapidly the while; takes out purse which he weighs in his hand*) The sinews of war to be_in with. What's this? a book! a diary! (*hurriedly turning leaves*) Queer notion—jotting down one's actions and ideas. (*thrusting it back in pocket with short laugh*) What a book *I* might have written! (*at the time the action of this scene has been going on he has been looking nervously to* R. *and* L.—*suddenly he starts, clutches up his garments from ground and retreats to rock; at same time roll of drum is heard close off stage, then a glad shout*) Nothing venture, nothing have. I've begun, and I'll go through with it; but first to get rid of—Silas Jarrett!

He disappears with body behind rock, L. U. E. *The rolling of drums continues, then a crowd of* SOLDIERS *and* CIVILIANS—*male and female—surges upon stage from various points, all in great excitement—*TRIGGS, POLLY *and* WATTLES *in their midst.*

POLLY. Our brave defenders! (*about to throw herself into* WATTLES' *arms—she is stopped by* TRIGGS, *who comes between.*)

TRIG. Excuse me, Miss Dobbs, but you're too expansive.

POL. What, would you have me restrain my feelings at such a time as this?

TRIG. Certainly not! let 'em overflow by all means—(*opening arms*) on me!

POL. Well, I'm so happy that I must hug somebody, so for once, Joe, it shall be you. (*she hugs him—all laugh*)

TRIG. Grateful woman! (*releases himself, and very grandly*) I am now rewarded for my exertions.

POL. Your exertions! (*all laugh*) But where is Sir Ormond Willoughby?

WAT. Yes, where's our brave colonel?

TRIG. ⎫
and ⎬ (*joyfully*). Here he comes!
POL. ⎭

Enter SILAS *as* SIR ORMOND, L. U. E., *and comes down,* C.

OMNES (*with wild delight*). The colonel! the colonel!

Movement—tableau. ALICE *rushes on from* L. 1 E., *and takes* SILAS JARRETT'S *hand.*

ALICE. Ah, you are safe—safe? Thank Heaven you are safe! (*tableau.*)

CURTAIN.

ACT IV.

ENGLAND.

SCENE I.—*Oakfield Grange,* MR. ST. CLAIR'S *house, near Southampton.*

POLLY *is busy with birdcage,* R., *hung against pavilion, into which she is put-*

tiny water and seed—rustic benches, seats, tables, etc., dispersed about stage.
TRIGGS, who is dressed in tweed suit and billy-cock hat, half-seated on
rustic table, his foot on bench.

TRIGGS. So you ain't gone to the races, Polly?

POL. (*sharply and without turning*). Judge for yourself, you can see me,
I suppose?

TRIG. Well, yours is not one o' them forms as requires a tourist's
telescope. (*rising and approaching her*) What makes you so snappish?
Here have I come over from Southampton a purpose to see you, and instead of saying "Joe Triggs, I am happy to have the honor," you insinu-
ates, "Joe Triggs, get out!"

POL. (*jumping suddenly off stool and falling against him, head on his
shoulder*). Joe! I ain't happy—far from it.

TRIG. (*with difficulty supporting her*). That's your fault! You might
be Mrs. Joe Triggs to-morrer.

POL. Yes, but I won't be Mrs. Joe Triggs, nor Mrs. Anybody else as
long as Miss Alice is so miserable. (*laying her hand confidentially on his
arm*) You know, Joe, she loves Mr. Arnold.

TRIG. And I know that Mr. Arnold is over head and ears in love with
her, but what of that?

POL. Simply that it can't be.

TRIG. Why can't it be? Is there a more faithful lovyer in the world,
except me? Why, when Mr. Arnold was brought wounded to the hos-
pital and nursed through his long illness by Mr. Jack, was there any
other name in his mouth but hers?

POL. He couldn't have a sweeter——

TRIG. And when we'd got him on his legs again and he learned that
Mr. St. Clair and Miss Alice, and yourself had departed for England,
didn't he sell up everything to follow her? And wasn't it only when
we got to Madras, that we learned that Sir Ormond Willoughby had sold
out and also left for England?

POL. (*mysteriously*) He's more than ever in love with Alice!

TRIG. What, Sir Ormond?

POL. Whether it was the siege, or the sea, or a sunstroke, or some
unpleasantness of that kind, but, of all the changed men Sir Ormond
Willoughby is the changest.

TRIG. Why?

POL. That's what I want to find out, as Mr. Jack used to say——

TRIG. Oh, don't talk of Mr. Jack to me! that's another thing as up-
set Mr. Arnold. No sooner had our ship touched England's shore, than
Mr. Jack disappeared, and though a month has elapsed, we've never
again clapped eyes on him.

POL. (*mysteriously*). P'raps he'd a sunstroke too! I hear they're
catching! But is Mr. Arnold coming to the luncheon to-day?

TRIG. Do you think he'd lose a chance of meeting Miss Alice?

POL. Then he'll meet Sir Ormond Willoughby as well, for the baro-
net joined Mr. St. Clair on the race course, and returns with him. But
what's the matter? You're not going, Joe?

TRIG. Yes, I am. (*aside, and moving up stage*). Better let Mr. Arnold
know of this—I left him at the inn, reading Miss Alice's letter.

POL. (*down stage*). You'd be sure to come back, Joe?

TRIG. To doubt it, Miss Dobbs, shows your ignorance of anatomy.
Where his heart is, there must Joe Triggs be.

As he turns to go up stage, he runs against ISAAC VIDLER, who, disguised as
a mendicant, is entering garden, C. He carries a walking-stick.

Beg pardon, but——

ISAAC. Please pity the poor blind—please pity!

TRIG. Polly, dear, if you've such a thing as a ha'-penny about you, give it him, and we can settle the account when we're married. (*bustles off at back as* POLLY *approaches* ISAAC, *who stands* C)

POL. (*giving money*). Have you been long blind, my poor man ?

ISAAC. D rk from my birth, your ladyship. Could never tell one color from an other—it's on'y by the feel (*slyly rubbing money*) that I know the vurld is green.

POL. (*at door of house*). You may rest on that seat till the guests arrive. (*as she exits into house,* VIDLER *opens first one eye, and then the other.*)

ISAAC. This is the splendacious crib ; and the servants are all out on the common, to see the people come back from the races. (*glancing slyly into pavilion*) There's vhere the luncheon's laid. Nobody took heed of the poor blind man, an' I spotted 'em carrying in the plate.

Music—looks cautiously round, gives a low whistle, which is answered by a cough, and the POLECAT *glides stealthily in at gate, and pauses up stage —he limps slightly.*

POLECAT. is it all serene, patri-arch ?

ISAAC (*impatiently*). Vy don't yer come quicker ? You'll have Jack Snipe here in a minnit or two interferin' with bis'ness.

POLE. (*limping slightly as he comes cautiously down*). If you'd have had a bullet in your leg for ten year, as I've had, your tongue wouldn't run so fast, to say nothin' of your other jinks. (*with a sudden and painful limp*) Ah ! (*clenching hand viciously*) When I comes across that Silas Jarrett !

ISAAC. Labor and vait, my blessed infant—labor and vait. Vot's the good o' vurritting ?

POLE. (*peeping into pavilion over* VIDLER'S *shoulder*). My eye! what forks and spoons !

ISAAC (*with trembling eagerness*). The 'all mark on everyone on 'em ! Ah, in such matters there's nothing like having to deal with the real gentle folk. (*coaxingly*) In vith yer, child of my 'art—in vith yer !

Urged on by ISAAC, *who keeps his two shaking hands on his shoulder,* POLECAT *is creeping cautiously towards door, when* JACK SNIPE *darts through open wicket,* C., *and with lightning rapidity glides between the two thieves to door of pavilion, he is dressed like a gipsy tramp.*

JACK (*fiercely*). Stow it, Polecat ; and you, patri-arch. I'm ashamed of yer. (*drawing himself up as they threaten*) Take the vally of a penny piece and I'd blow the gaff myself !

ISAAC (*still threatening*). Who'd lose by that ? We've our tickets, but you haven't yourn, my cherub !

JACK. Why, you'd lose one hundred pounds to begin with—that being the waluation they've kindly set on me for this ten year. Help me to carry out this one thing that I've set my 'art on, and you shall make that amount out of me ; do the other thing, and I walks to the nearest station and gives myself up at once. (*takes* C., *between them and looking from one to the other*) A hundred pounds is a large sum.

ISAAC (*with dignity*). A Vidler wouldn't sell his own father for less.

JACK. 'Spose I adds another hundred to the figger, and another hundred to that !

ISAAC. Yer takes my breath avay !

Jack (*grasping each by wrist and drawing them to him*). I've *seen* him! Both (*in same anxious whisper*). You don't mean——
Jack. Your enemy! my enemy! anybody's enemy! the ghost of the man I saw dead—dead. mind yer. dead! (*drawing back with a shudder—* Polecat, *who is sneaking behind, coughs—*Jack, *laying his hand quickly on* Vidler's *arm*) It's three hundred clear, mind yer! a winning game for you, it a losing one for me.

Music—passes rapidly up stage, and takes place by side of principal gateway, repeating the monotonous whine " Pity," etc., as Silas Jarrett, *in elegant morning costume—*Mr. St. Clair *and* Silas *enter at back.* l. c.—St. Clair *looking at his watch—*Silas, *as he comes through gateway, tosses money into* Vidler's *hat, but without looking at him, while* Vidler, *who has stooped so as to peer into his face, draws back with a start, and disappears quickly,* r. u. e.

Silas (*aside*). I like to scatter money—charity, after all, is but another name for ostentation, and it's a new feeling for me to be able to fling gold away. (*turns to* St. Clair, *who, as the* Ladies *exeunt by shrubbery,* r., *comes down stage—*St. Clair's *manner is grave and preoccupied—*Silas *is very grave and mercurial*) And when shall we fix the marriage day, St. Clair? business and pleasure, you know I'm all impatience till your charming little ward becomes my wife.
Clair (*coldly*). It will be for Alice to fix the day, Sir Ormond—I shall not force her inclinations.
Sil. Inclinations! Have you any reason to believe her *inclinations* are fixed elsewhere?
Clair (*with hesitation*). No, no positive reason, or frankly, Sir Ormond, I would give my sanction to the match. I'm under great obligations to you, Sir Ormond Willoughby—I am a man of business and know that such advances must be repaid.
Sil. When Alice Armitage becomes my wife I cancel all such obligations. (*airily*) It is but an affair with the lawyers, after all.
Clair (*warmly*). Excuse me if I differ, greatly differ with you. I fully recognize the position and noble name you offer my ward, but if such a marriage be against her will, the engagement is null and void.
Sil. (*with change of air*). It was my faith in that engagement being ratified that led me to extend the time for the re-payment of my advances. (*checking himself*) However, you have been more than a father to the young lady, and I'm sure when she quite understands your position she will render you the obedience of a daughter.
Clair. Speak to Alice yourself, she only can decide.

Confusion of merry voices, as from shrubbery. l., *two or three* Ladies *appear at entrance of shrubbery with croquet mallets.*

Ladies (*all together run on* l. c.). Mr. St. Clair! Mr. St. Clair!
First L. We are disputing terribly!
Second L. So you must come and be umpire! Sir Ormond will excuse you for a few moments.
Clair (*with forced laugh*). I am quite at your service. ladies. (*aside to* Silas *as he goes up*) I'll find Alice, I will send her to you, but, whatever the result, I leave her free as air. (Ladies *laughing and talking, surround* St. Clair—*they exeunt to shrubbery,* l. u. e.)
Sil. (*looking after him with changed manner*). St. Clair thinks the young lady is ignorant of his financial difficulties, but I've taken care that she should have the fullest information and know that the prosperity or

ruin of her benefactor rests entirely in her own pretty little hands. (*with change of manner*) Sir Ormond Willoughby, of Willoughby Court! (*exultantly*) It was a great game to play, and I've played it well! Oh, I could scream with ecstacy when I think that the law—the law! the eagle-eyed law has been baffl-d by the vagabond, Silas Jarrett, at last! (*checking himself with a start, then lowering his voice, with cautious look round*) I'm forgetting myself. (*with a laugh*) No! I'm remembering myself, which is just the thing I must avoid. (*confusion of female voices and laughter off stage,* L.) I'll join the croquet players—(*yawns*) I'm beginning to feel the *ennui* that belongs to a great name, besides, I'm beginning to grow fond of innocent amusements—they're so new to me.

Exits by shrubbery, L. U. E., *jauntily dusting boots with handkerchief, and humming an air —*ALICE *appears at back. She wears light summer walking costume. As she enters by* C. *gates, her hand is caught by* ROBERT ARNOLD, *who accompanies her —she withdraws it hastily, but without anger.*

ALICE (*coming down*). No, no—you must leave me—you must indeed! I'm not my own mistress, Robert!

ROBERT (*passionately*). True, you belong to me—your heart is mine, Alice, you cannot give it to another!

ALICE (*quickly*). No. Arnold, I will not attempt to deny it—I love you and have ever loved you with all my heart, and can picture no greater happiness than that of being your wife—I know the full extent of the sacrifice, but the sacrifice must be made.

ROB. (*bitterly*). And, of course, you do not hesitate to make it?

ALICE. Did Mr. St. Clair hesitate in my mother's need to make a sacrifice for her? An orphan and without a friend, has he not filled a parent's place to me?

ROB. He has.

Re-enter JACK SNIPE, C., *and hides behind tree,* L.

ALICE. And would you have me reproach myself in the midst of our happiness? (*placing her hand softly on* ROBERT's *arm and looking appealingly into his face*) That is, supposing, Robert, dear, that we were married—which we cannot be—would you have me reproach myself with the thought of his misery, of his ruin—a ruin which I might have prevented?

ROB. (*impetuously*) At the worst, it's but poverty!

ALICE. But poverty! ah, I know what poverty means—I saw and recognized its face when a child—a face as terrible as that dreadful one in the fable, which chills the warm blood in the veins, and changes all that is human in us into stone.

ROB. Sir Ormond Willoughby knew of our love, and he promised——

ALICE. Sir Ormond Willoughby is a changed man—to me, to all! So changed, that, at times, even his voice startles me, and I look up with doubt whether it can be the same man, once so generous and so good.

JACK (*aside*). Bless her! Young or old, one woman's worth twenty men, after all.

ROB. (*with passionate tenderness, drawing* ALICE *towards him*). Who could forego so sweet a prize? I admit the temptation, while I hate the man; but, my own darling, do not believe I will permit you to be erased thus from my life without a struggle. No, a thousand times no! I would not wish my worst enemy the torture I have felt since I received your last letter.

ALICE. Robert!

Rob. Mine is no common love, Alice! No love of yesterday. I have known you from a child—loved you from a child, I may say; for in all that long, dreary, awful time at Dartmoor, your innocent face was as a sunny memory that gave me hope even in the midst of my despair.

Alice (*her head unconsciously drooping on his shoulder*). Don't speak so, Robert, *don't speak so*

Rob. Oh, Alice, my one thought—my only thought for years—don't give me up, dear, don't turn away from me.

Alice (*suddenly breaking away from him*). Good-bye, say good-bye to me, Robert; you mustn't speak to me any more, you mustn't, indeed! (*sinking on garden chair, and waving him away as he would approach her*) I can't bear it, Robert. Leave me, leave me!

Rob. (*with sudden passion, as sobbing, she covers her face with her hands*). Leave you, yes; but lose you, Alice, never! (*moving up stage*) I will see this man—this man so false to his word, so changed in every way! It's not with tears and prayers that *I* will seek to move him, but as a man should speak to the man who would rob him of all he holds dear on earth.   [*Exit by shrubbery, L. 2 E.*

Alice (*springing to her feet*). Robert, Robert! (*moves up stage to follow him, when* Jack *glides rapidly between them.*)

Jack (*putting finger to his lips*). Don't shriek, miss! don't shriek! It's not for my sake, but your own, as I repeats, don't shriek!

Alice (*alarmed*). Who are you? What do you want?

Jack (*reproachfully*). No harm to you, Miss Alice, you can take your oath of that—quite contrarywise——

Alice (*forgetting everything in her delight, and speaking joyously*). Why, it's Jack! (*springing forward and seizing his hands*) Oh! I'm so glad to see you—but, why did you leave Mr. Arnold, and why did you leave me?

Jack (*quite overcome*). Bless you, miss, it wasn't for my own good, you may be sure—to think that you should condescend to know me again! right off, too! without any questions as to where I've been, or what I've been doing—but it's like you, miss, it's just like you.

Alice. But why *did* you leave Mr Arnold?

Jack (*seriously*). Becos he was in distress.

Alice (*drawing back*). Ah!

Jack. And becos I thought as I'd made a discovery, as I dussn't even whisper to anybody.

Alice. What discovery?

Jack (*gayly*). Oh, never you mind, missee, but I've come nigh strikin' a balance, an I that balance will be in your favor, though I carried over a thunde in' debt to some one else's account.

Alice. What do you mean?

Jack. Which meanin' shall be developed hereafter. (*while speaking, he has contrived that they shall approach door of house—voice heard in shrubbery —aside, quietly, and urging her into house*) Now you leave all this to me, miss. (*coaxingly*) You used to trust in Jack once, trust him now.

Alice. I will trust you!

Jack (*with growing excitement*). And I'll bring it through as sure as my name's Jack Snipe! Yes, that's my name, miss, and—*drawing back as she extends her hands*) I'd never touch those blessed finger tips again till I've done a something as may make you and Mr. Robert in after years, mind yer, say "he wasn't such a bad 'un after all."

As she exits into house, L., he crouches back for one moment as Silas Jarrett *and* Robert Arnold *enter from shrubbery. L. U. E., and come down stage—at the same moment the heads of* Vidler *and* Polecat *appear, as watching near gate, R. U E.—at a signal from* Jack *they disappear, and as* Silas *and* Arnold *continue to talk, he goes up stage and off, R. U. E.*

SILAS (*laughing*). A broken heart! Excuse me, Mr. Arnold, but talk to me of fear, cold, hunger, or any of those ailments by which men and women die by thousands and tens of thousands, but a broken heart is like broken china—the stronger when rivetted.

ROB. (*with passionate outburst*). Sir Ormond Willoughby, do you think I have forgotten the words you uttered in India, when you lay, as I thought, dying in my arms, and I was staunching the blood that was flowing from your breast?

SIL. (*who has slightly averted his face, now stands with his back half turned from* ARNOLD). What men say under such circumstances is often but the utterance of a momentary weakness. That I said something vaguely I am aware, but what the something was—perhaps you'll remind me?

ROB. The words you said were these—' Alice has spoken to me—I know all—all!' "

SIL. All what?

ROB. And Miss Armitage has herself told me of the promise you then so nobly made to her of resigning all pretension to a hand which——

SIL. (*interrupting*). Really, if ever I talked such sentimental nonsense I must have been raving, and I'm grateful to the bullet that recalled me to my senses. Alice wrongs her own attractions to think I could give her up so easily. (*he again insolently turns half away.*)

ROB. (*with fierce and passionate movement, lays hand upon his shoulder*). Sir Ormond Willoughby, you are a villain! a cold-blooded, heartless villain! The last of your name without a relation, and soon—I dare prophesy, to be without a friend; yet you do not shrink from blighting the future of two lives. (*suddenly pauses as* SILAS *savagely looks into his eyes—both for a brief moment gaze fixedly and menacingly at each other, then* ROBERT *staggers a step back, but immediately recovers himself, again grasps* SILAS, *this time by both shoulders, his eyes still rivetted on his face*) You are *not* Sir Ormond Willoughby! Your face is the face of the man I knew and loved, but your eyes—your eyes are the eyes of——

SIL. (*seizing* ARNOLD, *and casting him off*). Touch me again at your peril!

Simultaneous with this action, the croquet party come crowding on from shrubbery, L. U. E, *and* ALICE, *followed by* POLLY *from house, and* JOE TRIGGS, *from* R. U. E., *with two* OFFICERS, *who remain at back.*

CLAIR Sir Ormond! Robert! what's the meaning of this?

SIL. (*who has recovered his sang-froid*). The meaning is that Mr. Arnold forgets himself when he bandies words with a gentleman. (*taking c. of stage, he points to* ARNOLD, *who, pale with passion, has made a step towards him, but is held back by* ALICE, *who clings to his arm.*)

ALICE Robert! for my sake, for mine!

SIL. The social scale has indeed become a sliding scale, when ladies and gentlemen can hold companionship with a felon from Dartmoor! (*general movement.*)

CLAIR (*indignantly*). He was "Not Guilty!" (*with rapid look round*) He was not guilty!

SIL. Not guilty! the plea that every rascal sets up in the dock.

CLAIR. You know the man who robbed me was——

JACK (*bursting through company and laying his hand on* JARRETT'S *sleeve*). *Silas Jarrett!* That's the man! here's the man! (*by a quick movement he rips up* JARRETT'S *sleeve, and shows arm bare*) It is *tattooed*, read for yourselves, ' Silas Jarrett, traitor."

ISAAC (*who, with the* POLECAT *has come down, same time as* JACK—*one on either side of* SILAS). Which I tattooed myself at Dartmoor, with the help, and in t e presence of them all——

POLE. We swore you should be a marked man among us. (*in his ear*) A feller does\`t get a bullet in his hip for nothin'.

SIL. (*by a powerful effort throwing off* JACK SNIPE, *looks quickly from* VIDLER *to* POLECAT, *glances round to company, then draws himself up with usual mocking laugh*) My luck again! (*laying his hand on* JACK'S *shoulder*) But we're in the same trap, my *friend*—I go back to prison, but you go with me'.

JACK (*very brightly*). Proud an' 'appy, afore I entered on this bis'ness d'ye think I didn't reckon the consequences? (*stepping briskly forward*) Here, gentlemen, take and lock me up, but we shall make a nice comfortable rubber at whist. (*turning to* SILAS) I've won the game, haven't I? and I never doubted but I'd win it, when the stakes was—(*turning to* ALICE) your 'app ness, miss, and Mr. Robert Arnold's.

ROB (*grasping* JACK'S *extended, but trembling hand, and shaking it heartily*). You noble, generous, foolish fellow! had you not left me as you did, you would have known that a free pardon was obtained as a reward for your bravery in India.

JACK (*turning to* SILAS). Hallo! You'll have to go alone—sorry to break up the whist party.

ISAAC (*with a scream*). Vot! (*aside to the* POLECAT) Sold for the hundred!

ALICE (*taking* JACK'S *other hand*). And so you'll share our happiness.

TRIG. (*who has advanced with* POLLY *on his arm*). And ours!

SIL. (L., *about whom the* OFFICERS *have quietly gathered, as guarding him —h is taken out pocket-book, which he opens*). Mr. St. Clair, this is a full release, signed by the real Sir Ormond Willoughby—I found it among his papers (*tossing it, so that it falls at* ST. CLAIR'S *feet*) I bear you no malice—(*jauntily raising hat*) Good-bye, Miss Armitage! of all the assemble l company the only person I leave with any feelings of regret, is your charming self! (*as he turns to go up stage*, ROBERT *makes an angry movement, which is stopped by* ALICE, *who quickly interposes*)

ALICE. Robert! dear Robert! do not heed what he says! For my part, I am so happy at the thought that we shall never again be parted, that I can forgive *him!* Forgive him with all my heart! (ROBERT *clasps her to his breast, while* JACK *bursts into a rapid double shuffle of delight. The rest of characters group —*SILAS, *up stage, regarding scene us*)

CURTAIN DESCENDS.

SYNOPSIS.

THE play begins in a street at Southampton, at one corner of which is visible the interior of a large room in the house of TRUMBLE, a solicitor, who is visible to the audience, writing at a desk. In the street WATTLES, a recruiting sergeant, is busy trying to get recruits. One TRIGGS, having the appearance of a shabbily-dressed lawyer's clerk, enters. The sergeant seeks to entice him, but the shilling device is "too thin" for TRIGGS. The recruiting party all leave, except the sergeant and drummer, when TRIGGS is accosted by POLLY DOBBS, who comes forward and affects surprise at seeing TRIGGS still there. The girl proceeds to tell him that she is certainly going to India with Mrs. Dr. McTAVISH; bids him good-bye! promises to return, as she quits the stage. TRIGGS utters an amusing speech, half humor, half satire, as he departs, leaving the soldiers singing inside the neighboring tavern. Then TRUMBLE rises from his chair, and comes to the window, grumbling at the noise made by the soldiery. ROBERT ARNOLD, in the dress of a journeyman lock-smith, comes on. He appears to be a great favorite, as the soldiers and others surround him. He tells them that he has also joined the army, and is going to sail with them to India as confidential clerk to CAPTAIN WILLOUGHBY. TRUMBLE, murmuring at the delay of TRIGGS, says that he had better meet Mr. ST. CLAIR half-way, and disappears. At this moment SILAS JARRETT, a gipseyish-looking tramp, appears; he is clad in ragged but showy clothes. The company are laughing loudly, and he bitterly curses them all, especially ROBERT ARNOLD—"honest, hardworking Robert, who's always mocking me with his pity." He draws up under the shadow of the wall as TRUMBLE passes along without noticing him. Suddenly he affects to be drunk, as he is noticed by others. POLLY says, "Is not that Silas Jarrett?" "Yes, drunk as usual," is the reply. SERGEANT WATTLES asks if any of them had ever noticed his wonderful resemblance to CAPTAIN ORMOND WILLOUGHBY. They had. SILAS staggers around, listening to everything going on. ROBERT recognizes him, and gives him his last half-crown; then the whole party go off to parade the streets, except Silas, in whose face POLLY shuts the door. MARGARET ARMITAGE, in widow's weeds, enters, and implores SILAS to help her, as her little girl is dying of hunger. The wretch shakes her off, entering the tavern, just as ROBERT ARNOLD comes on singing mirthfully. He catches sight of MARGARET, who has fallen to the ground, and lifts her up, then ejaculates, "Why are you here, and crying?" She feebly tells him that little ALICE is starving. ROBERT becomes sobered in an instant. He assists the woman to her lodgings, and promises to supply her pressing needs. Hardly has he left the stage before SILAS enters, and finds ARNOLD's basket of tools, among them some skeleton keys; while he hides as he hears steps approaching, and conceals himself. Soon TRUMBLE and Mr. ST. CLAIR enter. SILAS overhears the latter tell the lawyer that as he leaves for India in the morning, he wishes him to take possession of a note case, and give the contents to any surviving members of the Armitage family—who were, in equity, the owners of it. TRUMBLE enters his office to put away the note case, watched by SILAS, while ST. CLAIR remains outside smoking. ROBERT enters, and impulsively appeals to ST. CLAIR for charity, and, after some hesitation, the latter gives him a five pound note. ROBERT runs off to use the note for Mrs. ARMITAGE, as SILAS stealthily enters TRUMBLE's office, and with ROBERT's tools abstracts the note case. In the next scene ROBERT enters the wretched garret of the ARMITAGES, carrying a basket of provisions. A cry of "Stop thief" is heard outside. SILAS just appears on the stage, sees ROBERT through a glass door in back room, and recoils. SILAS has the note case in one hand and the skeleton keys in the other. The crowd are heard outside as SILAS crams the notes into his breast, throws the keys and note case on the table, dropping purposely a ten-pound note. Then he disappears behind an old counterpane that conceals the wide fireplace. The crowd, headed by TRUMBLE and a policeman, rush in, confront ROBERT, and, finding every evidence of guilt, take him off, handcuffed. TRIGGS, who has enlisted to be with his POLLY, when he hears of ROBERT ARNOLD's arrest, would willingly fly to aid him, but martial law compels him to embark and leave his innocent friend to his fate. In Scene IV., which is terribly effective, SILAS gets drunk on board a packet ship, and gets into an altercation with ST. CLAIR, who finds him in possession of the notes he had left with TRUMBLE. An alarm is given—a scuffle—and SILAS avoids arrest by taking a "header" into the sea.

In Act II. ROBERT ARNOLD is working as a convict; JACK SNIPE, a very bad man with a very good heart, has taken a liking to him, and though, like himself, a convict, advises him to beware of a spy, nicknamed the POLECAT, and of the new warden, SILAS JARRETT! Mrs. ARMITAGE, ST. CLAIR, and the GOVERNOR pay a visit to the prison; where Mrs. ARMITAGE sees and recognizes ARNOLD, whom she and ST. CLAIR intend to get pardoned. But meanwhile an insurrection of the convicts takes place, and, although SILAS fires at ARNOLD, he escapes; but the former's cap falling off in the melee, he is recognized and denounced by ST. CLAIR.

In Act III. the scene changes to a military station on the banks of the river Jumna, in India. SERGEANT WATTLES, TRIGGS, and POLLY are together, and from them, midst a good deal of merriment and love-making, we learn that Miss ALICE ARMITAGE is living there under the care of Mrs. McTAVISH, and that SIR ORMOND WILLOUGHBY—now a Colonel—has proposed for the young lady's hand. An attack on the station by the insurgents is momentarily feared, and Miss ALICE has escaped from her chamber, by the aid of JACK SNIPE, the assistant of Mr. ROBERT ARNOLD, who has worked himself into a prominent position by his ability and good conduct. ALICE tells ARNOLD that she will appeal to COL. ORMOND WILLOUGHBY to give her up, and consent to her wedding him. She does so, and the noble soldier consents. Meanwhile the enemy has approached—a fight ensues; ARNOLD behaves heroically, and JACK SNIPE fights beside him, and even TRIGGS becomes inflamed with martial ardor. At this moment, when the men have all rushed to the front, SILAS, haggard, ragged, and footsore, crawls into the verandah. Events pass rapidly now. COLONEL WILLOUGHBY is killed, and ARNOLD goes for re-inforcements. SILAS finds the officer's body, and, remembering his likeness to him, robs him of his uniform; finding a diary in the coat pocket. He determines to personate the COLONEL, and succeeds, in the hurry attending the ending of the successful fight, in passing for him, and soon after leaves India for England.

In Act IV. all our characters have returned "home." SILAS (known as the COLONEL) insists upon wedding ALICE; ST. CLAIR wishes otherwise. A meeting is to take place at Mr. ST. CLAIR's mansion. While SILAS is carrying matters with a high hand, JACK SNIPE arrives, having followed him, and penetrated his disguise. He is denounced and seized, and ARNOLD is rewarded for his misfortunes by the hand of ALICE, while POLLY becomes the happy wife of her faithful TRIGGS.

EXPLANATION OF THE STAGE DIRECTIONS.

The Actor is supposed to face the Audience.

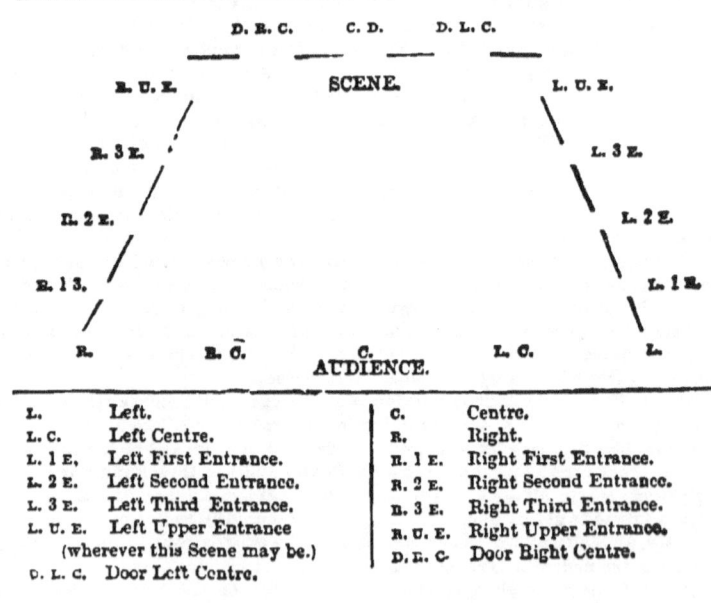

L.	Left.	C.	Centre.
L. C.	Left Centre.	R.	Right.
L. 1 E.	Left First Entrance.	R. 1 E.	Right First Entrance.
L. 2 E.	Left Second Entrance.	R. 2 E.	Right Second Entrance.
L. 3 E.	Left Third Entrance.	R. 3 E.	Right Third Entrance.
L. U. E.	Left Upper Entrance	R. U. E.	Right Upper Entrance.
	(wherever this Scene may be.)	D. R. C.	Door Right Centre.
D. L. C.	Door Left Centre.		

DE WITT'S
ETHIOPIAN AND COMIC DRAMA.

"Let those laugh now who never laughed before,
And those who always laughed now laugh the more."

Nothing so thorough and complete in the way of Ethiopian and Comic Dramas has ever been printed as those that appear in the following list. Not only are the plots excellent, the characters droll, the incidents funny, the language humorous, but all the situations, by-play, positions, pantomimic business, scenery, and tricks are so plainly set down and clearly explained, that the merest novice could put any of them on the stage. Included in this catalogue are all the most laughable and effective pieces of their class ever produced.

*** In ordering, please copy the figures at the commencement of each play, which indicate the number of the piece in "DE WITT'S ETHIOPIAN AND COMIC DRAMA."

☞ Any of the following plays sent, postage free, on receipt of price—
15 Cents Each.   Address,

CLINTON T. DE WITT,
No. 33 Rose Street, New York.

☞ The figures in the columns indicate the number of characters—M. *male*, F. *female*.

No.		M.	F.
73.	African Box, burlesque, 2 scene	5	0
107.	Africanus Bluebeard, musical Ethiopian burlesque	6	2
43.	Baby Elephant. sketch, 2 scene	7	1
79.	Barney's Courtship, musical interlude, 1 act	1	1
42.	Bad Whiskey, sketch, 1 scene.	2	1
6.	Black Chap from Whitechapel, negro piece	4	0
10.	Black Chemist, sketch, 1 scene	3	0
11.	Black-ey'd William, sketch, 2 scenes	4	1
40.	Big Mistake, sketch, 1 scene..	4	0
78.	Bogus Indian, sketch, 4 scenes	5	2
89.	Bogus Talking Machines (The) farce, 1 scene	4	0
24.	Bruised and Cured, sketch, 1 scene	2	0
108.	Charge of the Hash Brigade, Irish musical sketch	2	2
35.	Coal Heaver's Revenge, negro sketch, 1 scene	6	0
41.	Cremation, sketch, 2 scenes...	8	1
12.	Daguerreotypes, sketch, 1 scene	3	0
53.	Damon and Pythias, burlesque, 2 scenes	5	1
63.	Darkey's Stratagem, 1 act....	3	1
110.	De Black Magician, Ethiopian comicality, 1 scene	4	2
111.	Deeds of Darkness, Ethiopian extravaganza, 1 act	6	1
50.	Draft (The), sketch, 1 act.	6	0
64.	Dutchman's Ghost, 1 scene...	4	1
95.	Dutch Justice, sketch, 1 scene	11	0
67.	Editor's Troubles, farce, 1 sce.	6	0
4.	Eh? What is It? sketch	4	1
96.	Elopement (The), farce, 1 scene	4	1
52.	Excise Trials, sketch, 1 scene.	10	1
25.	Fellow that Looks Like Me, interlude, 1 scene	2	1
51.	Fisherman's Luck, 1 scene....	2	0
88.	First Night (The), Dutch farce, 1 act	4	2
106.	Gambrinus, King of Lager Beer, Ethiopian burlesque, 2 scenes	8	1
83.	German Emigrant (The), sketch 1 scene	2	2
77.	Getting Square on the Call Boy, sketch, 1 scene	3	0
17.	Ghost (The), sketch, 1 act....	2	0
58.	Ghost in a Pawnshop, 1 scene.	4	0
31.	Glycerine Oil, sketch.	4	0
20.	Going for the Cup, interlude..	4	0
82.	Good Night's Rest, 1 scene. ..	3	0
86.	Gripsack, sketch, 1 scene......	3	0
70.	Guide to the Stage, sketch....	3	0
61.	Happy Couple, 1 scene........	2	1
23.	Hard Times, extravaganza, 1 scene	5	1
3.	Hemmed In, sketch	3	1
48.	High Jack, the Heeler, 1 scene	6	0
68.	Hippotheatron, sketch........	9	0
71.	In and Out, sketch, 1 scene...	2	0
33.	Jealous Husband, sketch	2	1
94.	Julius, the Snoozer, 3 scenes .	7	0

No.		M.	F.
103.	Katrina's Little Game, Dutch act, 1 scene	1	2
1.	Last of the Mohicans, sketch..	3	1
36.	Laughing Gas, sketch, 1 scene.	6	1
18.	Live Injun, sketch, 4 scenes...	4	1
60.	Lost Will, sketch	4	0
37.	Lucky Job, farce, 2 scenes....	3	2
90.	Lunatic (The), farce, 1 scene..	3	0
109.	Making a Hit, farce, 2 scenes..	4	0
19.	Malicious Trespass, 1 scene....	3	0
96.	Midnight Intruder (The), farce, 1 scene	6	1
101.	Mollie Moriarty, Irish musical sketch, 1 scene	1	1
8.	Mutton Trial, sketch, 2 scenes	4	0
44.	Musical Servant, sketch, 1 sce.	3	0
49.	Night in a Strange Hotel, sketch, 1 scene	2	0
22.	Obeying Orders, sketch 1 scene	2	1
27.	One Hundredth Night of Hamlet, sketch	7	1
30.	One Night in a Barroom, sketch	7	0
76.	One, Two, Three, 1 scene	7	0
87.	Pete and the Peddler, Negro and Irish sketch, 1 scene	2	1
9.	Policy Players, sketch, 1 scene	7	0
57.	Pompey's Patients, interlude, 2 scenes	6	0
65.	Porter's Troubles, 1 scene	6	1
66.	Port Wine vs. Jealousy, sketch	2	1
91.	Painter's Apprentice (The), farce, 1 scene	5	0
92.	Polar Bear (The), 1 scene	4	1
14.	Recruiting Office, sketch, 1 act.	5	0
45.	Remittance from Home, sketch, 1 scene	6	0
105.	Rehearsal (The), Irish farce, 2 scenes	4	2
55.	Rigging a Purchase, sketch, 1 scene	3	0
81.	Rival Artists, sketch, 1 scene.	3	0
26.	Rival Tenants, sketch	4	0
15.	Sam's Courtship, farce, 1 act..	2	1
59.	Sausage Makers, 2 scenes	5	1
80.	Scenes on the Mississippi, 2 scenes	6	0
21.	Scampini, pantomime, 2 scenes	6	8
84.	Serenade(The), sketch,2 scenes	7	0
38.	Siamese Twins, 2 scenes	5	0
74.	Sleep Walker, sketch, 2 scenes	3	0
46.	Slippery Day, sketch, 1 scene.	6	1
69.	Squire for a Day, sketch	5	1
56.	Stage-struck Couple, 1 scene..	2	1
72.	Stranger, burlesque, 1 scene... and 2 children.	1	2
7.	Stupid Servant, sketch, 1 scene	2	0
13.	Streets of New York, 1 scene.	6	0
16.	Storming the Fort, 1 scene....	5	0
47.	Take it, Don't Take It, 1 scene	2	0
54.	Them Papers, sketch, 1 scene.	3	0
100.	Three Chiefs (The), 2 scenes ..	6	0
102.	Three A. M., sketch, 2 scenes.	3	1
34.	Three Strings to One Bow, sketch, 1 scene	4	1
2.	Tricks, sketch	5	2
104.	Two Awfuls (The), 1 scene....	5	0
5.	Two Black Roses, sketch	4	1
28.	Uncle Eph's Dream, 2 scenes..	3	1
62.	Vinegar Bitters, sketch, 1 scene	6	1
82.	Wake Up, William Henry....	3	0

No.		M.	F.
30.	Wanted, a Nurse, 1 scene	4	0
75.	Weston the Walkist, Dutch sketch, 1 scene	7	1
93.	What Shall I Take ? farce, 1 act	8	1
20.	Who Died First ? 1 scene	3	1
97.	Who's the Actor ? farce, 1 scene	4	0
93.	Wrong Woman in the Right Place, sketch, 2 scenes	2	2
85.	Young Scamp, sketch, 1 scene.	3	0
112.	The Coming Man, sketch, 1 act	3	1
113.	Ambition, farce, 2 scenes	7	0
114.	One Night in a Medical College, sketch, 1 scene	7	1
115.	Private Boarding, comedy, 1 scene	5	1
116.	Zacharias' Funeral, farce, 1 scene	5	0
117.	Motor Bellows, comedy, 1 scene		
118.	Helen's Funny Babies, burlesque	6	8

DE WITT'S ACTING PLAYS (Continued).

No.		M.	F.
44.	Lancashire Lass, melodrama, 5 acts	12	3
34.	Larkins' Love Letters, farce, 1 act	3	2
37.	L'Article 47, drama, 3 acts	11	5
11.	Liar (The), comedy, 2 acts	7	2
19.	Life Chase, drama, 5 acts	14	5
35.	Living Statue (The), farce, 1 act	3	2
48.	Little Annie's Birthday, farce, 1 act	2	4
32.	Little Rebel, farce, 1 act	4	3
34.	Little Ruby, drama, 3 acts	6	6
99.	Locked In, comedietta, 1 act	2	2
35.	Locked In with a Lady, sketch, 1 act	1	1
87.	Locked Out, comic scene	1	2
43.	Lodgers and Dodgers, farce, 1 act	4	2
89.	Leap Year, musical duality, 1 act	1	1
63.	Marcoretti, drama, 3 acts	10	3
54.	Maria and Magdalena, play, 4 acts	8	6
63.	Marriage at Any Price, farce, 1 act	5	3
39.	Master Jones' Birthday, farce, 1 act	4	2
7.	Maud's Peril, drama, 4 acts	5	3
49.	Midnight Watch, drama, 1 act	8	2
15.	Milky White, drama, 2 acts	4	2
46.	Miriam's Crime, drama, 3 acts	5	2
51.	Model of a Wife, farce, 1 act	8	2
84.	Money, comedy, 5 acts	17	3
08.	Mr. Scroggins, farce, 1 act	3	3
88.	Mr. X., farce, 1 act	3	3
69.	My Uncle's Suit, farce, 1 act	4	1
30.	My Wife's Diary, farce, 1 act	3	1
92.	My Wife's Out, farce, 1 act	2	2
193.	My Walking Photograph, musical duality, 1 act	1	1
140.	Never Reckon Your Chickens, etc., farce, 1 act	3	4
115.	New Men and Old Acres, comedy, 3 8	5	
2.	Nobody's Child, drama, 3 acts	8	3
57.	Noemie, drama, 2 acts	4	4
104.	No Name, drama, 5 acts	7	5
112.	Not a Bit Jealous, farce, 1 act	3	3
185.	Not So Bad as We Seem, play, 5 acts	14	3
84.	Not Guilty, drama, 4 acts	10	6
117.	Not Such a Fool as He Looks, drama, 3 acts	5	4
171.	Nothing Like Paste, farce, 1 act	3	1
14.	No Thoroughfare, drama, 5 acts and prologue	13	6
173.	Off the Stage, comedietta, 1 act	3	3
176.	On Bread and Water, farce, 1 act	1	2
90.	Only a Halfpenny, farce, 1 act	2	2
170.	Only Somebody, farce, 1 act	4	2
33.	One too Many for Him, farce, 1 act	2	3
3.	£100,000, comedy, 3 acts	8	4
97.	Orange Blossoms, comedietta, 1 act	3	3
66.	Orange Girl, drama, in prologue and 3 acts	18	4
172.	Ours, comedy, 3 acts	6	3
94.	Our Clerks, farce, 1 act	7	5
45.	Our Domestics, comedy farce, 2 acts	6	6
155.	Our Heroes, military play, 5 acts	24	5
178.	Out at Sea, drama in prologue and 4 acts	16	5
147.	Overland Route, comedy, 3 acts	11	5
156.	Peace at Any Price, farce, 1 act	1	1
82.	Peep o' Day, drama, 4 acts	12	4
127.	Peggy Green, farce, 1 act	3	10
23.	Petticoat Parliament, extravaganza, in one act	15	24
62.	Photographic Fix, farce, 1 act	3	2

No.		M.	F.
61.	Plot and Passion, drama, 3 acts	7	2
138.	Poll and Partner Joe, burlesque, 1 act	10	3
110.	Poppleton's Predicaments, farce, 1	3	6
50.	Porter's Knot, drama, 2 acts	8	2
59.	Post Boy, drama, 2 acts	5	3
95.	Pretty Horse-Breaker, farce, 1 act	3	10
181 and 182.	Queen Mary, drama, 4 acts	38	8
157.	Quite at Home, comedietta, 1 act	5	2
196.	Queerest Courtship (The), comic operetta, 1 act	1	1
132.	Race for a Dinner, farce, 1 act	10	
183.	Richelieu, play, 5 acts	16	2
38.	Rightful Heir, drama, 5 acts	10	2
77.	Roll of the Drum, drama, 3 acts	8	4
13.	Ruy Blas, drama, 4 acts	12	4
194.	Rum, drama, 3 acts	7	4
195.	Rosemi Shell, travesty, 1 act, 4 scenes	6	3
158.	School, comedy, 4 acts	6	6
79.	Sheep in Wolf's Clothing, drama, 1	7	5
37.	Silent Protector, farce, 1 act	3	2
35.	Silent Woman, farce, 1 act	2	1
43.	Sisterly Service, comedietta, 1 act	7	2
6.	Six Months Ago, comedietta, 1 act	2	1
10.	Snapping Turtles, duologue, 1 act	1	1
26.	Society, comedy, 3 acts	16	5
78.	Special Performances, farce, 1 act	7	3
31.	Taming a Tiger, farce, 1 act	3	
150.	Tell-Tale Heart, comedietta, 1 act	1	2
120.	Tempest in a Teapot, comedy, 1 act	2	1
146.	There's no Smoke Without Fire, comedietta, 1 act	1	2
83.	Thrice Married, personation piece, 1 act	6	1
42.	Time and the Hour, drama, 3 acts	7	3
27.	Time and Tide, drama, 3 acts and prologue	7	5
133.	Timothy to the Rescue, farce, 1 act	4	2
153.	'Tis Better to Live than to Die, farce, 1 act	2	1
134.	Tompkins the Troubadour, farce, 1	3	2
165.	Turning the Tables, farce, 1 act	5	3
168.	Tweedie's Rights, comedy, 2 acts	4	2
126.	Twice Killed, farce, 1 act	6	3
56.	Two Gay Deceivers, farce, 1 act	3	
123.	Two Polts, farce, 1 act	4	4
198.	Twin Sisters (The), comic operetta, 1 act	3	1
162.	Uncle's Will, comedietta, 1 act	2	1
106.	Up for the Cattle Show, farce, 1 act	6	2
81.	Vandyke Brown, farce, 1 act	3	3
124.	Volunteer Review, farce, 1 act	6	6
91.	Walpole, comedy, 3 acts	7	2
118.	Wanted, a Young Lady, farce, 1 act	3	
44.	War to the Knife, comedy, 3 acts	5	4
105.	Which of the Two? comedietta, 1 act	2	10
98.	Who is Who? farce, 1 act	3	2
12.	Widow Hunt, comedy, 3 acts	4	4
5.	William Tell with a Vengeance, burlesque	8	2
136.	Woman in Red, drama, 3 acts and prologue	6	
161.	Woman's Vows and Mason's Oaths, 4 acts	10	4
11.	Woodcock's Little Game, farce, 2	4	4
54.	Young Collegian (Cantab.), farce, 1	3	3

ACTING PLAYS.

RECENT ISSUES.

www.ingramcontent.com/pod-product-compliance
Lightning Source LLC
Chambersburg PA
CBHW030859260626
47169CB00008B/2597

* 9 7 8 3 3 3 7 3 4 3 7 7 4 *